William Seton

A glimpse of organic life, past and present

William Seton

A glimpse of organic life, past and present

ISBN/EAN: 9783741187827

Manufactured in Europe, USA, Canada, Australia, Japa

Cover: Foto ©Andreas Hilbeck / pixelio.de

Manufactured and distributed by brebook publishing software
(www.brebook.com)

William Seton

A glimpse of organic life, past and present

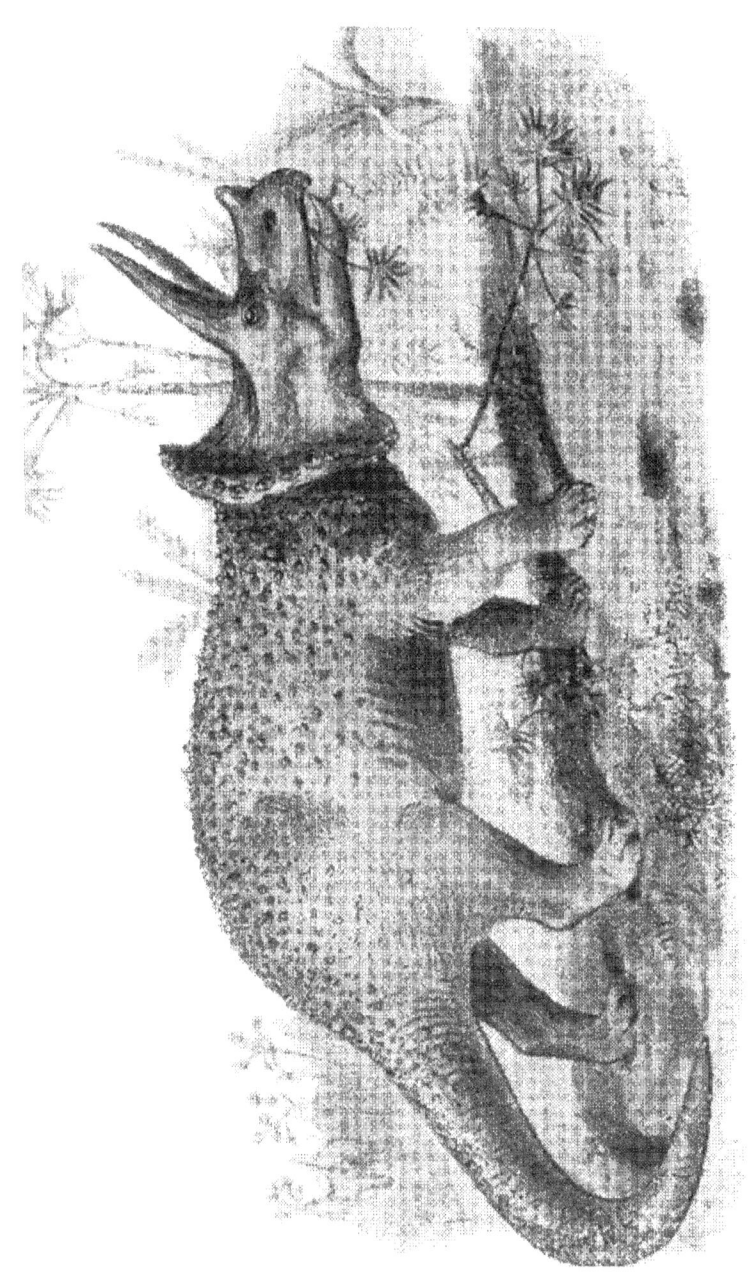

HORNED DINOSAUR.

Frontispiece.

A

GLIMPSE OF ORGANIC LIFE:

PAST AND PRESENT.

BY

WILLIAM SETON, LL.D.

NEW YORK:

P. O'SHEA.

19 BARCLAY STREET.

TO THE VENERATED MEMORY

OF

THE VERY REV. JOHN McCAFFREY, D. D.

MANY YEARS

PRESIDENT OF MT. ST. MARY'S COLLEGE.

"Si proche que Dieu soit de la nature, il ne se confond pas avec elle, car l'histoire du monde nous révèle une unité de plan qui se poursuit à travers tous les âges, annonçant un Organisateur immuable, tandis que la paléontologie nous offre la spectacle d'êtres se modifiant sans cesse. . . . . Le changement paraît être la suprême loi de la nature. Il y a quelque mélancolie dans le spectacle de ces inexplicables disparitions. L'âme du paléontologiste, fatiguée de tant de mutations, de tant de fragilité, est portée facilement à chercher un point fixe où elle se repose; elle se complaît dans l'idée d'un Être infini, qui, au milieu du changement des mondes, ne change point."—
Albert Guadry: Essai de Paléontologie Philosophique,
page 211.

In the beginning God created.

" But overpoweringly strong proofs of intelligent and benevolent design lie all around us, and if ever perplexities, whether metaphysical or scientific, turn us away from them for a time, they come back upon us with irresistible force, showing to us through nature the influence of a free will, and teaching us that all living beings depend upon one ever-acting Creator and Ruler.—*Closing sentence of Sir William Thomson's presidential address to the British Association, Edinburgh, 1871.*

"Ni l'apparition successive des types ni leur enchaînement ne sont en opposition avec l'enseignement de l'église. . . . Il suffit aux évolutionistes pour rester Catholiques de respecter deux dogmes essentiels ; la création primitive de l'univers et une nouvelle intervention du créateur pour donner à l'homme une âme douée de raison et appelée à l'immortalité."—*Le Présent et l'Avenir du Catholicisme en France, par l'Abbé de Broglie, p. 113.*

PREFACE.

DEAR READER:

THIS little book is the fruit of many happy hours. Beginning with the far off Past, it traces briefly the development of organic life through the Ages, and we shall consider ourselves well repaid, if, besides giving a little pleasure and instruction, it may kindle in you a love for the neglected study of Natural History.

This study makes the world we live in so much more interesting. The wild flower blooming by the wayside and the bee hovering around it, will appeal to us as never before when we know that they are allies: that insect life and plant life are closely bound together. And the birds, which come back to us in spring-time, will be watched and welcomed with a keener delight when we learn their habits: how they live and keep house and bring up their little ones. And after we have looked with an intelligent eye on the birds and flowers and insects, we may discover that the very rock on which we are seated is a book vastly older than the oldest book in our library; it may contain within itself the records of a past geological epoch, when animated nature was very unlike what we see it to-day, and when Man had not yet come upon the scene to rule—but sometimes, alas, to ruin—the joy and glory of the landscape.

W. S., LL.D.

To L. P. Gratacap, M. A. of the Museum of Natural History, New York, the author's thanks are due for his kindness in reading through the text and giving valuable information with respect to late fossil discoveries.

The skeletons of the Greenland' whale and of the Archæopteryx are taken from *Romanes' Darwin, and After Darwin,* by permission of the Open Court Publishing Company.

CONTENTS.

A GLIMPSE OF ORGANIC LIFE:

PAST AND PRESENT.

CHAPTER I.

THE ROCKS.

IT was a June morning and I was strolling along a high, rocky field which commanded a broad view of the surrounding country, accompanied by William Smith, my favorite pupil. I call him thus, for like myself he was fond of nature. The birds were singing merrily, countless butterflies were flying hither and thither, and bumble-bees and grasshoppers helped to give life and joy to the scene.

"How beautiful all this is!" exclaimed William. "How much better to be here than shut up in a class-room. And to-day, Professor, you were going to begin and tell me

something about the earth and the creatures
that live upon it.''

'' Yes, but you must be patient, for it is a
long story.''

'' And yonder is a bed of moss, Professor.
Let us sit there and I will listen to you with all
my ears.''

We did so, and presently I began. '' We
sometimes hear it said, William, that between
natural science and religion there is an antago-
nism which obliges us to give up the one or
the other. This is not true. If we believe that
the earth and all that lives upon it is the work
of Almighty God and that He has given to Man
a soul destined to immortality, we may—hold-
ing fast to these two truths—advance with
fearless step in the study of the Creator's work.
But while it is a fascinating study, it is also a
difficult one, for in order to understand the
plants and the animals which exist to-day, we
must begin with the ones which existed ages
ago, and the history of those far off ages is

recorded in a singular and extremely ancient book; it is folded and hidden in the rocks, and I must therefore begin and tell you something about this book of the rocks."

"Book of the rocks!" murmured William.

"Yes, and now let me ask you what is a rock?"

"Why, something very, very hard like this," and he thumped his heel on a slab of granite which skirted the edge of the moss.

"Such is indeed the common acceptation of the word, William, but in scientific language any material, be it sand or clay, that forms a portion of the earth's crust, is considered to be rock quite as much as this granite; for what is hard to-day may in time, by exposure to the air, disintegrate and become dust: and vice versa, materials which to-day are soft, may become hard, just as common mortar does, which we might call artificial rock."

"This is new to me, Professor, and I cannot imagine how such materials, whether hard or soft, can tell us anything about the earth's life-history."

I smiled and went on. "All rocks, William, may be broadly divided into two classes, namely, *stratified* and *unstratified*. Unstratified rocks are those which have been melted by heat, and consequently we learn from them very little of the organic development of life : they are blank pages as it were, and are sometimes termed *igneous* rocks; and geologists believe that the greatest part of the earth's crust which lies *beneath* the surface is composed of them.   The granite which you struck with your foot a moment ago is a good type of the unstratified class; and after telling you that the minerals of which granite is mainly composed are *quartz*, *feldspar*, and *mica*, I pass on to the stratified rocks.   Stratified rocks are so called from the strata or layers which subdivide them.   The greater part of the earth's surface is covered by these rocks, of which there are three kinds, sand rocks, clay rocks, and lime rocks, which pass by degrees one into the other. And here let me observe that it was a namesake of yours—William Smith— who first discovered the importance to natural history of stratified rocks. At the opening of our century he was employed in England to lay out new highways and to make canals, and he perceived that each stratum of earth was characterized by different fossils. Now, these fossils served as nothing else could to distinguish the different periods of the earth's history. So do not forget your great namesake."

"I will not, and I am prouder than ever to be called William Smith."

"And now be very attentive to what I am going to say about stratified rocks, for so much of what we know of the life-history of the earth depends upon them. These rocks may also be called *sedimentary*, for they are in reality nothing but sediments deposited in ancient lakes and seas. Now, in these sediments animals and plants of various kinds were slowly laid down

and preserved—we might say sealed up—and
then brought to light in after years when the
waters retired and left the sea or lake bottom
uncovered. But during the time when the
land was free from water it of course had no
sediments deposited on it, and consequently
there were no organisms sealed up and preserved as fossils; and whenever this has hap-
pened, a part of the record is said to be lost—
a leaf has been torn out of the book. Of
course animals and plants were living during
the time the land was bare of water, but since
they could not become fossilized (except so far
as they were carried by floods into distant lakes
or seas), they are not represented. Then when
from some cause the land again became sub-
merged and sediments began to form anew, the
remains of animals and plants began again to
be deposited: but we generally find them a
little different from the former plants and animals from which they are separated by an
almost horizontal plane running across the face

of the rock and thus making two distinct strata. So bear in mind, William, that whenever we meet with stratified or sedimentary rocks, we know that at some period water has covered that part of the earth."

"Well, Professor, is any dead animal or plant a fossil?"

"No, in order to be termed a fossil it must belong to a species that is extinct and have existed at a former geological epoch.* But before I proceed I wish you to look well at this big sheet of paper on which I have broadly divided the history of the earth into four ages, and I have named each age from its dominant type." Here I unrolled the sheet and spreading it out on the moss I asked William to read aloud what was written on it, beginning at the bottom, for the lowest rocks are the oldest.

---

* Strictly speaking, any entombed, or even exposed, skeleton—vertebrate or invertebrate—which has partially lost its original constitution by solution, is a fossil.

A TABLE OF GEOLOGICAL AGES.

(Each Age named from its Dominant Type.)

AGE OF MAMMALS.
- Man.
- Equus.
- Elephas—Bison—Llama.
- Pliohippus.
- Protohippus.
- Mastodon.
- Miohippus.
- Mesohippus.
- Dinoceras.
- Serpents—Monkeys.
- Orohippus.
- Eohippus.
- Most generalized Mammal: Phenacodus Primaevus.

REPTILES.
- Chalk.
- Birds with teeth: Hesperornis—Ichthyornis.
- Earliest Mammals: Marsupials.
- Ancestral Bird: Archaeopteryx.
- Flying Reptiles: Pterodactyls.
- Reptiles: Dinosaurs, etc.

INVERTEBRATES.
- Fern-like plants of immense size; vegetation abundant.
- Earliest Amphibians: Labyrinthodonts.
- Coal.
- Insects: Beetles–Cockroaches–Centipedes–Spiders.
- Cartilaginous, armored fishes; abundant.
- Fish-like forms.
- Low forms of Seaweed.
- Nautili: Corals—Sponges—Worms—Crinoids.
- Trilobites: abundant.

ARCHAEAN.—Fossils doubtful.

CHAPTER II.

ARCHAEAN AGE AND AGE OF INVETEBRATES.

WILLIAM: "Before you begin, Professor, to speak about the animals and plants of the different geological ages, may I ask a question?"

"Certainly you may."

"Well, you said yesterday that the fossil remains found in newer and higher strata were as a general rule more or less unlike the ones found in older strata immediately below. Pray what caused animals and plants to become unlike?"

"Before I give you the opinions of naturalists upon this subject, William, let me repeat and beg you not to forget that we do indeed as a general rule, to which there are exceptions, find all animals and plants gradually changing as we ascend from lower to higher strata. You

know that the time unrepresented in the geological record was a time when the land was
free from water, and when consequently no
sediments were being deposited in which organic
remains could be sealed up and preserved as
fossils. Now, this period unrepresented was
no doubt a period when physical geography and
climates were different: and the Creator has
wisely allowed the living things He created to
change along with changing external influences,
otherwise they must surely all have perished.
But this adaptation to a new environment does
not imply that the animals and plants changed
all of a sudden. We do not know how long it
took them to change; and if sometimes in the
geological record the modifications appear to
come about abruptly, it is probably only because we are ignorant of the transition forms
which existed during the period unrepresented,
and when, as I have said, the earth was free
from water and when therefore no organic
remains could be preserved as fossils."

"Well, I should like to know, Professor,
what may have been the natural law — sanc-
tioned by the Creator—whereby modifications
in plants and animals have come about."

" Ah, many minds have been at work to
discover that law, William, and it is now the
general opinion of naturalists that the successive development of life, the modifications of
organic forms from low to higher types, have
come about in one of two ways, or perhaps by
the two ways combined. Some eminent men
believe that it is the habits, the mode of life,
which has produced the modifications we perceive in studying the fossils in the rocks.
According to them, marked changes in surrounding conditions have brought about changes
in the habits of animals, and new habits have
caused the use of new parts, and this, after a
time, has resulted in the production of new
organs and a modification of the old ones:
and these changes have been transmitted by
inheritance to succeeding generations, until in

the course of time—perhaps after many thousand years—the ancestor and its far off descendant have grown to be very different one from the other. Other naturalists, eminent men too, lay stress on the fact that as many more plants and animals come into existence than are able to reach maturity, those among them which possess any variation that is beneficial (a bird, for example, having stronger wings, keener eyes) will stand a better chance to live than the ones not so favored, and this beneficial variation being handed down to the offsping, will in the course of generations—through the unending struggle to become better adapted to surrounding conditions (and as a rule surrounding conditions are always more or less changing and offering a premium on every favorable variation), will cause the animal or plant little by little to depart from the original type, until the remote descendant grows to be very unlike its ancestral form.''

"How interesting!" exclaimed William. "And now I can understand how in a natural way animals and plants have been allowed by the Almighty to become quite different from the original ones which were created in the beginning."

"And when, by and by, William, you study geology and learn how many times in the history of the earth land has become water and water has become land, and how climates have changed, you will be more impressed than ever with the necessity for plants and animals to have been able to adapt themselves to a changed environment: it was either that or utter extinction. But I myself, William, am inclined to believe that the factors of development which I have mentioned are not sufficient: I believe there is something wanting, and that we have to allow a certain share in the process of change to the senses of the lower animals. In my opinion, the knowledge which they obtain through the senses has been allowed by the

Creator a wider range than we are generally willing to concede. Now, the wit* of the lower animals—if I may thus express myself—exercised ages ago by the ancestral forms in the direction of safety, may have led certain favored ones among them to acquire new and beneficial habits, so as to meet and become adapted to changed conditions of life. And these initial, beneficial habits, thus acquired and transmitted through heredity, may have counted for something in organic development."

"Well, I see that you have divided the history of the earth into four parts," said William, smiling, perhaps at what I had been saying, and bending over the geological map which was spread out on the moss.

"Yes, and the age of Invertebrates, as well as the age of Reptiles and the age of Mammals, may be separated into a number of epochs

* May not the bird which flutters round and pretends to be wounded and thus draws you away from her nest, have learned from experience that the trick may sometimes succeed?

which I have not marked: it will be time enough to study those epochs when you take up geology."

"Well, I see, Professor, that in the lowest and oldest age, the Archaean, you have written—'Fossils doubtful.'"

"I have done so because we have no good evidence that organic life existed when those rocks were laid down."

"That must have been very, very long ago," said William.

"Yes, millions of years, and we find patches of these most ancient rocks in various parts of the United States, while they cover a large portion of Canada and Labrador. It would, however, be rash to say that the rocks of the Archaean age actually form the primitive crust of the earth. They may be merely the oldest rocks we know, the first leaves, blank leaves, belonging to geological history, all the letters of which have been effaced."

"Well, in the age immediately following

the Archaean—in the age of Invertebrates—I see many signs of life," said William.

"Yes, and please bear in mind that each age may be known by its characteristic fossils: bear in mind, too, that as we ascend from the lowest and the oldest to the highest and the newest strata through all geological history, we find organic life, with some exceptions, grow‐ ing more and more complex in structure, more perfect, more fitted for Man, the last and most perfect of all God's works, to live among: Man did not appear until the earth was worthy to receive him."

"Well, you say, Professor, that there were some exceptions. Pray, why did not all living creatures change with time? Why have any remained stationary?"

"Because the influences which affected them have remained constant: they have not been exposed to an intense struggle. And these ex‐ tremely ancient forms—such as the very rare *Pearly Nautilus*; a marine shell-fish, the

Lingula; a microscopic deep-sea animal, the *Foraminifera*, and a few others, which are about the same to-day as they were millions of years ago, are known as *persistent types*, and these persistent types usually live in deep water or burrow in sand along the seashore, and their tenacity of life is very great."

"Oh, now I understand," said William, "the stationary condition of a few species is owing to the fact that there has been no motive power to cause them to change."

"Precisely."

"Well, I see, Professor, that the first animals you have marked on the map are called Invertebrates; this means, I believe, animals without a backbone?"

"Yes, and we discover at the very opening of the age of Invertebrates many signs of life: the life system is distinctly recorded. I shall not, however, burden your memory with the names of the different classes to which these early invertebrates belonged: enough to know

that the sea bottom swarmed with a fauna of
low degree—with sponges, corals, nautili, crinoids, worms, and trilobites: and let me especially call your attention to the trilobites, whose
bodies, as the name indicates, were divided
into three parts. The broad head-plate of this
crustacean was no doubt useful for burrowing
and hiding in the slimy ooze, and among the
animals of the first part of this distant age it
ranked the highest. It is also interesting to
know, William, that this primeval invertebrate
is most nearly represented in our day by the
common horseshoe, or king crab, which is a
divergent crustacean branch.''

"Well, why do you call the trilobite a
crustacean, Professor?''

"Because its skin was hardened and crust-
like: crabs, lobsters, and shrimps are also
crustaceans.''

" And did it live in the sea?''

"Yes, and it was like its nearest living
affinity — the horseshoe crab — essentially a

water-breather. But in that far off age there was not much dry land."

"A water-breather! I never heard that expression before."

"I mean, William, that the trilobite was able to breathe under water by means of gills—just as a fish does. The water passing through the gill-slits supplies the blood-vessels round about them with the oxygen needful for life. And let me observe that it is very interesting to study the influence of oxygen in water. All the outward parts of an animal which come in contact with a medium full of oxygen, form, as it were, a breathing surface, and any internal portion of an animal may also become a breathing surface, provided the medium containing oxygen can reach it. But the part or parts which seem best fitted to breathe are those to which the term 'organs of respiration' is properly applied. It has been proved that in many invertebrate animals the mucous membrane of the intestinal canal serves for

breathing, and we know that gills may occur
in the intestine of a water animal as well as on
the outer surface. In some species of water-
lice gills are found as appendages to the legs,
while other invertebrates, the common leech
for instance, breathe only through the skin.
In fact, William, there is no hard and fast line
between water-breathers and air-breathers: and
you will see by and by that some fish can pass
a good part of their time out of water, while
a frog when not allowed to come to the surface, may live under water as long as it is
given food and is plentifully supplied with fresh
water: here skin respiration takes the place
of lung respiration. The physiological action
of the air-breathing organs of animals living in
air does not differ from that of the skin and
gills in water-breathing animals. Through
them the blood is brought into the nearest contact with the medium containing oxygen. Yet
nothing can be conceived more unlike in structure than a fish's gills, the lungs of the higher

vertebrates, and the tracheae of insects. The tracheae of insects, William, are exceedingly fine elastic tubes ramifying in all directions and allowing the alternate inspiration of fresh air and expiration of impure air: and by these tiny tubes the oxygen needed is brought directly to and absorbed by all the organs of the insect. But I did not intend to give you a lesson in physiology, so let me end these remarks by asking you to read carefully a book which I shall lend you: it is by Professor Karl Semper and is entitled 'Animal Life as Affected by the Natural Conditions of Existence.' "

"I thank you, sir, and I promise to read it very carefully." Then after a pause: "But you said, Professor, that along with trilobites there were corals living at the beginning of the age of Invertebrates: pray tell me something about corals."

"Well, a coral, properly speaking, is a very small aquatic animal belonging to the class of Polyps. This little creature is able to extract carbonate of lime from sea water and deposit it within the lower part of its own body, leaving the upper part free to move about: * and what are known as coral reefs and coral islands are merely the limestone accumulations of millions of dead coral-polyps. And it is interesting to know that a large portion of the State of Florida has been formed by coral-polyps.''

'' Indeed! And pray, sir, what is that? It looks like a little flower on the map.''

'' That, William, is a crinoid: an aquatic plant-like animal, which in the seas of the Invertebrate age lived rooted to the bottom; it was held there by a jointed stalk. It is sometimes called a sea-lily, and a fossil specimen has been found whose stem was nearly sixty feet long. At the present day this animal, when full grown, is not attached to the bottom, but moves freely about.''

---

* It is more strictly correct to say that, as a rule, coral polyps are sclerodermic, and deposit the lime at the mesenteric divisions.

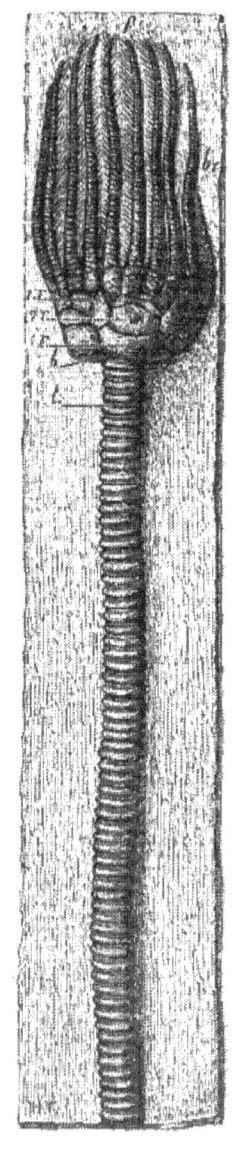

Page 34.

A CRINOID

"And I see, Professor, that there were also sponges among those early invertebrates. Really, I did not know that a sponge was an animal?"

"But it is one; and no animal living in the sea is so interesting. The sponge gets its food from microscopic organisms which are constantly streaming in through all its pores while it remains fastened to the bottom. And here let me quote what Professor Alexander Agassiz says: 'All our ordinary notions of individuality, of colonies, and of species are completely upset. It seems as if in the sponges we had a mass in which the different parts might be considered as organs capable in themselves of a certain amount of independence, yet subject to a general subordination, so that we are dealing neither with individuals nor colonies in the ordinary sense of the word.'"

"Well, I shall think of this the next time I use my sponge," * said William, smiling.

* The bath sponge is merely the skeleton.

"There were," I continued, "other animals besides invertebrates living at this early period, but as invertebrates were by far the most numerous they have given their name to the age."

"Well, I see hardly any plants marked on this part of the map, Professor."

"There was comparatively little dry land at that period, William, and so there could not have been much vegetation. We do find, however, a few club mosses and low forms of seaweed. But we must remember that in all the ages, plants are not so commonly found in a fossil state as animals, for the reason that vegetable tissue is much more perishable than the hard parts of an animal."

"Ah, true, and I wonder, Professor, if this part of the globe was under water during the Invertebrate age."

"It was nearly all under water, but our own good State of New York, as well as New England, was above the sea, and geologists believe that the shore line extended a good deal farther to the east than now. There was also some dry land far to the west, in the region of Colorado, while north of us was a great V-shaped land-mass, one arm of which lay in what is to-day British Columbia, and the other arm extended to Labrador. There is evidence too to show that our continent developed from the north towards the south."

"And did all these primeval invertebrates continue to be as abundant as time went on, Professor?"

"Yes, all except the trilobites. These before the age closed became much fewer. They had already passed their prime and they finally disappeared; but while the coral-polyps and other aquatic invertebrates continued to abound, they, as we know from fossil remains, became somewhat unlike the earliest ones, and this change of species, William, you will find going on, with some exceptions as I have already told you, through all geological time."

"Well, Professor, here is something that I might almost take for a fish on your map."

"Yes, this earliest vertebrate, that is to say, an animal with a backbone, and which good authorities believe to have been a fish, appears as you perceive, towards the middle of the Invertebrate age, and some authorities maintain that the ancestral fish is to-day represented by a small fish-like animal not quite two inches long, called Amphioxus.* Certainly no other vertebrated animal yet discovered is of such an archaic type. It has only a rudimentary backbone (and embryology shows that a temporary dorsal axis of this kind is found in all vertebrates soon after the beginning of embryonic life). It has no brain, no limbs, no ears; one pigmented spot represents the eye, and it has about a hundred gill-slits."

* "The Amphioxus . . . is generally regarded as the ancestral vertebrate. There are many reasons why this position must be accepted, although it possesses a few secondary modifications."—COPE: *Primary Factors of Organic Evolution.*

"Well, a little higher on the map, Professor, I see marked: 'Fishes Abundant.'"

"Yes, a little higher in the geological strata fossil remains of fishes become plentiful. Indeed, the second half of the Invertebrate age might be called the epoch of fishes, and I need hardly say, William, that the life system has now made a great step in advance, for low no doubt as the ancestral fish was, a vertebrate marks a higher form of life than an invertebrate: but these early fishes differed a good deal from the fishes of our day. In the first place, they all had soft, cartilaginous skeletons, and if so many of their fossil remains have been preserved in the rocks, it is thanks to the close-fitting, enameled scales or plates which enveloped them like armor. Their tails, too, differed in shape and structure from the tails of modern fishes. In fact, they were not typical fishes, but may be viewed as connecting forms, that is to say, that along with true fish characters they combined other characters which linked them

to higher vertebrates, such as the amphibian
Labyrinthodonts, whose fossil remains are discovered in a little later and higher geological
horizon; but as we proceed with our history of
the life-system the rocks will reveal to us many
such *generalized*, connecting types, anticipations, as it were, of an epoch that is approaching.''

"Well, generalized is a new word to me,
Professor.   Pray, what does it mean?''

" In natural history, William, a type is said
to be generalized when it combines within itself
characters not only belonging to its own branch,
or we might say to its own root, but also characters appertaining to allied branches, and
which afterwards become distinctive of higher
types.''

"Ah, now I understand the word.   And
let me ask another question, sir.   Was the land
surface increasing all the time?''

" Yes, the presence of more land is indicated by the greater number of plants.   There

are now many fern-like trees of great size. Insects too appear on the scene, and among them we find beetles, cockroaches, centipedes and spiders."

"And what is the meaning of this broad, dark line on the paper, Professor?"

"It indicates the first appearance of coal, and shows that we have arrived at the last division of the age of Invertebrates, which division is known as the carboniferous epoch, when probably nine-tenths of all the coal in the world was accumulated."

"And just above the dark line you have drawn a curious looking animal, Professor."

"It is the earliest amphibian. By an amphibian I mean an animal which when very young breathes exclusively by gills, but afterwards by lungs, either alone or associated with gills. A frog is an amphibian and so is a salamander. It has also other characteristics, which I need not give at present."

"Well, Professor, what really is coal?"

"Coal is the remains of extinct plants and trees. As we have advanced in geological time, the land surface has been increasing, comparatively low, swampy land, and towards the close of the age of Invertebrates the vegetation was extremely rank. Coal-mines abound with roots and stumps of various kinds, and naturalists believe that it was now that the great classes of the vegetable kingdom began to diverge. And, as I remarked awhile ago of the primeval fishes, namely, that they were *generalized*, connecting types, so were these carboniferous plants and trees intermediate forms which connected classes that in our age are widely apart. No other conclusion can be drawn by anyone who carefully studies the coal vegetation, and it is interesting to know that this vegetation indicates everywhere a moist, tropical climate. Let me say also that the carboniferous division of the Invertebrate age may be viewed as essentially an air-purifying one. Carbonic acid was withdrawn from the atmosphere and stored up in vegetation preserved as coal, while at the same time the air became better supplied with oxygen needful for higher forms of life. Thus we see, William, how the earth was becoming all the time better fitted for Man, although Man was not to appear until long after this age."

"And what is the name, sir, of this primeval amphibian?"

"It is called a Labyrinthodont, from the labyrinthine structure of its teeth, and it was a species of salamander. Labyrinthodonts differed a good deal in size and appearance. The one which I have represented was discovered in Bavaria. It was about forty-two inches long. It had paddles instead of feet, and its general form shows that it was adapted to a fish-like existence. These amphibians were first found in hollow fossil trees in Nova Scotia, and such trees are often met with in coal-mines."

CHAPTER III.

THE AGE OF REPTILES.

"WE have now arrived at another geological age, William, the age of Reptiles. Of course invertebrates and cartilaginous fishes continue to be very plentiful, but reptiles have become the dominant type, and though like amphibians they are cold-blooded, owing to the peculiar character of their circulating system, still they mark an advance in organic life, for reptiles breathe by lungs and never by gills, and we may view them as transition forms leading up to the lowest mammals. But unless the story of the rocks greatly misleads us, the age of Invertebrates did not come to an end without terrible movements of the earth's crust. A large portion of the land area disappeared under water. Much animal and vegetable life was

destroyed and the coal formations lay hidden
for a time under a shroud of sand and gravel.
Then when the waters receded and the drowned
land came in sight again, the eye rested on a
very different landscape. In place of low,
swampy, carboniferous jungles, we behold shallow estuaries and mountains; and in our own
country, William, the Appalachian chain has
risen up, and this upheaval is sometimes known
as the Appalachian revolution. The opening of
the age of Reptiles was a great transition period
for animals and plants. Since the environment
had so much changed, since the geography and
climates were no longer the same, organic life
had to adapt itself to very different conditions,
and it is interesting to find in the rocks of this
period so many transition forms, while occasionally we meet with old types and new types,
amphibian Labyrinthodonts and true lung-
breathing reptiles side by side in the same geological formation. But although the first reptiles
were, as we might expect, generalized, connect-

ing forms, they soon reached a high scale of organization, and never before nor since in the world's history have their numbers been so great as in this age to which they have justly given their name.''

'' Well, what is this little animal, Professor, which you have placed just above the earliest reptiles ? ''

'' It represents the earliest mammal, and although the ancestral forms of this the highest class of animals were of a low, reptilian type, they mark another advance in the life system. And now, William, I wish you to remember, for it is important, that the mammal class is divided into two great groups, each group being provided with milk-glands — mammae — by which the young are nourished with milk after birth. But in one group, which is much the larger, when the embryo has reached a certain stage of development, a connection is formed between the mother and it, which connection is called the placenta, and the whole embryonic development takes place *within* the womb. In the other and much the smaller group, there is no such connection between the mother and the embryo, and the young one leaves the womb in a very imperfect state. The former are called placental-mammals, the latter, non-placental. Now the earliest mammals to appear in geological time belonged to the inferior, non-placental group, and if we view these primeval mammals isolated and by themselves, they are enigmas to us; but when we view them in the light of embryology and palaeontology, we see in them the intermediate, transition forms leading up to the larger group, the typical mammals, which appeared somewhat later, and whose young, as I have said, come forth in a perfect state." *

"And are any of these primitively organized mammals existing to-day, Professor?"

"Yes, our opossum belongs to this lowly,

* See "*Les Ancêtres de nos Animaux dans les Temps géologiques.*"—By ALBERT GUADRY. Prof. de Paléontologie au Museum d'Histoire Naturelle. Paris.

non-placental group. We may look upon it as
a survival; and in Australia, which has been
aptly named the fossil continent, all the mammals excepting the bats, and those introduced
by man, are non-placentals. But now, William,
it is time to come back to the reptiles, for this
is their age, you know.''

"Oh, yes, and do tell me a great deal about
them, sir.''

"The first reptile of which I shall speak is
the Ichthyosaurus, which is chiefly found in
Europe, and is represented in our country by
the Mosasaurus. It had a wide geographical
range, for its fossil remains have been met with
in Australia as well as north of the Arctic
Circle. Its body was not unlike a whale's. It
had a fish-like tail, a triangular fin on the back,
two pairs of paddles, and its mouth was full of
large, conical teeth, sometimes two hundred in
number. This shark-like fish-lizard, as it may
be called, grew to be twenty, and even forty feet
long, and being a true reptile, that is to say an

THE ICHTHYOSAURUS.

air-breather, it was obliged now and again to rise to the surface for a fresh supply of oxygen. Those who have given most study to the subject believe that the ichthyosaurus, like the whale, in the beginning lived a good part of the time on land, and certain features in the skull, vertebrae, and teeth point to a descent from the amphibian labyrinthodonts.

" And let me add, William, that it is chiefly to the American scientists Marsh, Cope, and Leidy that we owe our knowledge of this remarkable reptile, which, as I have said, is represented in North America by the Mosasaurus, and which abounded in the shallow sea that flowed during a part of the Reptile age through the middle of our continent. Professor Cope tells us how strange it was to find the remains of these animals, at one time so plentiful between the Missouri and the Rocky Mountains, now lying stranded a thousand miles from the nearest tide-water. In the report to the U. S. Geographical Survey of the Territories, Vol. II.,

1875, he says: 'If the explorer searches the bottoms of the rain-washes and ravines he will doubtless come upon the fragments of a tooth or jaw, and will generally find a line of such pieces leading to an elevated position on the bank or bluff where lies the skeleton of some monster of the ancient sea. He may find the vertebral column running far into the limestone rock that locks him in his last prison, . . . or a pair of jaws lined with horrid teeth, which grin despair on enemies they are powerless to resist,' etc. Along with the Ichthyosaurus, and leading much the same kind of existence, was another reptile called the Plesiosaurus. But its head, instead of being large, was small like a lizard's head, and it had a long, slender, snake-like neck. Specimens have been found which measure forty feet, and good authorities believe that, like the Ichthyosaurus, it was descended from a terrestrial or semi-aquatic ancestor, whose structure underwent a good deal of

PLESIOSAURUS.

AN ARMOURED DINOSAUR.

Page 51.

change in the process of adaptation to a life in the water."

"And I see on your map, Professor, a reptile that looks a little like a crocodile."

"It is meant to represent a Dinosaur, a name derived from two Greek words meaning 'terrible lizard.' Dinosaurs were the highest in the scale of reptiles, for they possessed characters which connected them with mammals and also with birds, but they were not all monsters like this one. They varied a great deal in size and in shape, as do all animals with a wide geographical range. Some were not bigger than a cat, while others exceeded the dimensions of an elephant, and were encased in bony plates and spines, and some even had horns. Perhaps no naturalist has thrown so much light on this extinct order of Reptiles as Professor Marsh of Yale College, whose discoveries in the far west are world-known. But, as I have said, there were different species of Dinosaurs, and this one on which you have placed your finger be-

longs to the kind known as the Atlantosaurus,*
a thigh bone of which and some parts of the
vertebral column were found in the Rocky
Mountains; and this thigh bone, which in the
largest living crocodile is only twelve inches
long, measures seventy-two inches. We may
therefore not unreasonably picture to ourselves
a reptile eighty feet long, and this would make
the Atlantosaurus the largest land animal that
ever existed.

"But probably a more formidable member
of the order than the Atlantosaurus was the
Tricerotops, for, if its length was only twenty-
five feet, it was armed with a pair of horns
which measured thirty-six inches.

"But the Dinosaur known as the Megalosaurus must have been more formidable still, if
indeed it had any rivals among these ancient
reptiles. Its length was thirty feet, its jaws
were full of saber-like teeth, which show that

* In the American Museum of Natural History, New
York City.

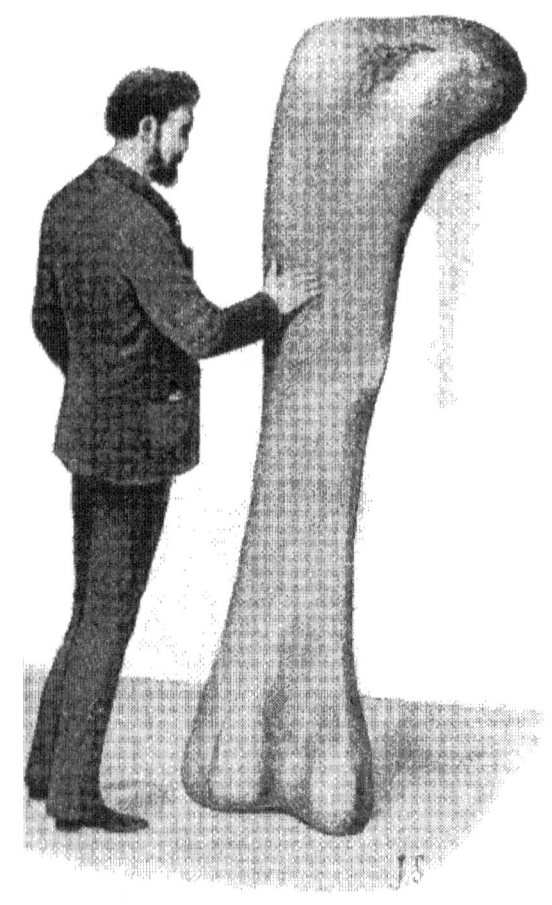

THIGH BONE OF ATLANTOSAURUS.

Page 52

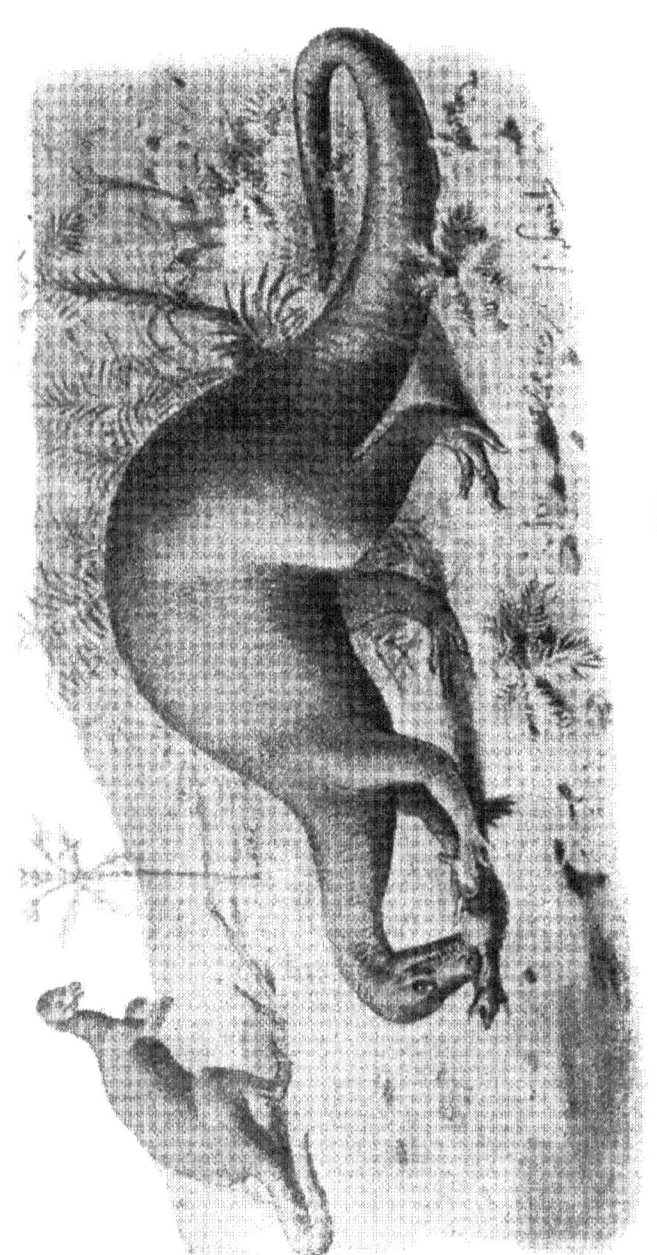

MEGALOSAURUS.

Page 53.

it was a flesh-eater, and its great kangaroo-like hind legs, upon which it probably stood erect, must have enabled it to make terrific bounds after its prey. And let me add, William, that the fossil footprints in the Connecticut Valley, which at first were thought to be bird tracks, are now generally believed to have been made by these creatures.''

"And here you have drawn something that looks a little like a bird," said William.

"Yes, this reptile, the Pterodactyl, had wings and is sometimes called a flying-lizard. Some Pterodactyls were not bigger than a robin; others measured twenty-five feet from wing tip to wing tip. Properly speaking, its organ of flight was not a typical wing, but a smooth, thin, leathery membrane, somewhat like the wing of a bat, only not supported in the same way. Of the bat's five fingers, four are used to support the wing and only one is free; while in the Pterodactyl only one finger supports the wing and four are free and end in

sharp claws. In the flying-lizard we see combined the long, flexible neck, and hollow air-
filled limb bones characteristic of birds, with
the head and jaws of a reptile. But all were
not armed with teeth, and their uncommonly
big eyes would indicate that their habits were
nocturnal. Some day, William, I shall take
you to the Yale College Museum and show you
Marsh's collection of Pterodactyls, the largest
in the world and numbering over six hundred
specimens.''

"And this tiny thing flying beside the
Pterodactyl, what may it be, Professor?"

"It represents the earliest butterfly."

"And quite near the butterfly is a bird,
is it not, Professor?"

"Yes, the earliest bird. And it appears,
as you see, towards the close of the Reptile age.
But this primitive bird, of which there are
only two specimens, and which is named *Archaeopteryx*, differs in some important respects
from the birds of to-day. It is not a typical

PTERODACTYLS

"And what is its name, Professor ?"

"It is called a Lemur, and from it the monkey is descended."

"Well, near to the lemur you have drawn on the map something like a huge fish, sir."

"It may look like a fish, but it is not a fish. It is a whale-like mammal called the Zeuglodon. In Georgia and Alabama the fossil remains of this immense creature, which was probably sixty feet long, are very plentiful. Now, the Zeuglodon is interesting because, according to good authorities, it is the transition form which connects the Whale group—namely, the whales, porpoises, and dolphins—with the other mammals. And you no doubt know that these warm-blooded fish-like creatures suckle their young, like other members of the Mammal class, and they are obliged now and again to rise to the surface in order to breathe."

"No, sir, I thought the whale was a fish."

"But it really is not one, William. The whale's fore limbs have become modified into a

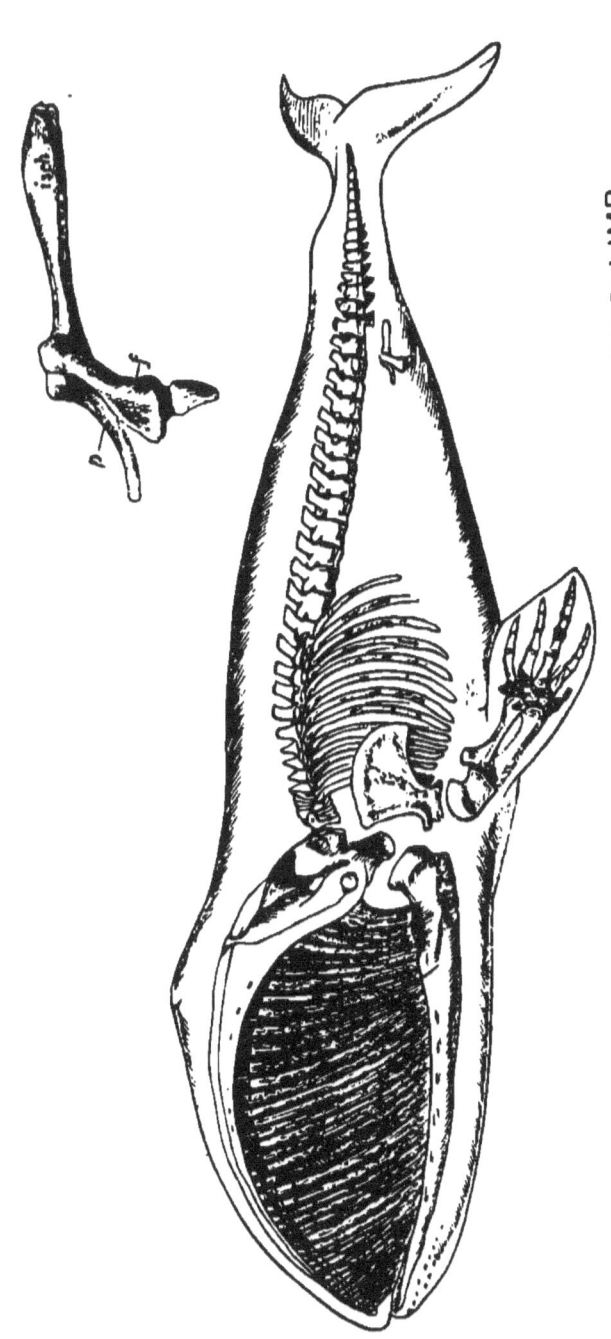

'age 65.   SKELETON OF WHALE SHOWING RUDIMENT OF HIND LIMB

Taken from " Darwin and after Darwin " by permission of the Open Court Pub. Co.

pair of flippers, but they reveal the typical bones of a true mammalian limb; while its hind limbs have quite disappeared externally, and are found internally in only one species, namely, the whalebone-whale, where faint traces of them are discovered deeply buried in the muscles. Even the whale's head, so like the head of a fish, retains all the bones of the mammal skull in their proper anatomical relations one to the other."

"You said hind limbs, Professor. Well, do you really believe that this fish-like animal ever walked on the land ?"

"What other conclusion can we draw, William? The whole structure of the whale goes to show that its progenitor was a terrestrial quadruped of some kind. And let me add that if this mammal's blood does not become chilled by the water in which it now lives, it is owing to the layer of fat which encloses nearly its whole body."

"And is this the earliest snake?" said

William, pointing to an animal on the map very near the first lemur and the ancestral whale.

"Yes, and like the whale, it also had legs at one time."

"Indeed," said William.

"Not a vestige remains of the snake's fore limbs," I continued. "But in one species, the Python, we do discover tiny rudiments of the hind limbs."

"Well, how did snakes come to lose their legs, Professor ?"

"It was probably brought about, as in the Whale group, by changed conditions of life. When under the influence of natural causes an organ becomes useless to any animal, it will in the course of generations dwindle away, and sometimes disappear altogether, at least externally ; it becomes what is termed a rudiment."*

* Some writers, whose forte is not natural science, explain the rudiments of hind limbs in the Baleen whale and the python, by saying that the Creator placed these dwarfed and useless structures there merely for the sake of adhering to an ideal type. We might ask why the

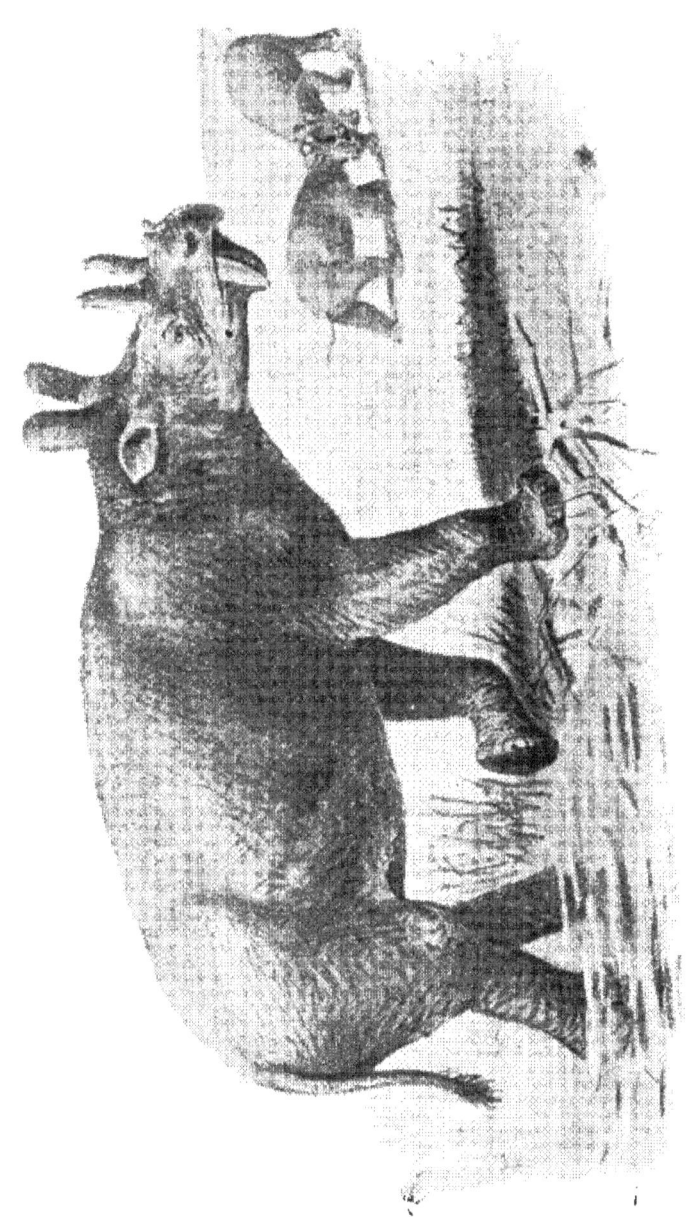

THE DINOCERAS.

Page 67.

"And a little above the earliest snake, sir, you have placed a very big animal. Pray, what may it be?"

"It is called the Dinoceras, and it may possibly be the ancestor of our greatly modified elephant.* Judging by its fossil remains, which were discovered by Marsh in Wyoming, in 1870, the Dinoceras had somewhat shorter legs than the elephant, and it is calculated that when alive it weighed between two and three tons. On its skull we find six bony elevations, which may indicate six true horns; but this is uncertain. It had also in the upper jaw two dagger-shaped tusks: but well armed as it was the Dinoceras must have been a stupid beast, for no other

Creator formed these little legs in only one species of whale and in only one species of snake, and why He formed only two legs instead of four. Doubtless these writers are ignorant of the fact that the distinguished American palaeontologist, Professor Cope, has traced the Ophidian order back to reptiles of the Permian epoch, which reptiles have well developed limbs.

* See in American Museum of Natural History, New York City.

mammal living or extinct had so small a brain
in proportion to its bulk. Yet in this respect,
namely, smallness of brain, it resembled all the
early mammals. The progress of mammalian
life is well illustrated by the brain growth; it
furnishes the key to many other changes.''

"And what is this other beast, Professor,
which must have been very big too, if I may
judge by your drawing of it, and which you
have placed in a little higher and later geological strata? ''

"It is called the Brontops, and it appeared,
as you see, not very long after the Dinoceras,
which it surpassed in size. Its height was
eight feet, and its length was twelve, and when
it came on the scene the great interior lakes
had been drained off, and in place of vast,
dreary marshes, there were beautiful upland
prairies.''

"And in the same strata with the Brontops, we discover an animal, William, which
reminds us a little of the Eohippus, but it is

BRONTOPS.

SKELETON OF BRONTOPS.

Page 69

larger and more horse-like. The feet especially
have changed to meet altered conditions, for
the Miohippus has to roam over harder ground,
and look at it well, for it is one of the links in
the development of the horse.''

"And living at the same period as the
Brontops and the Miohippus, Professor, I see
on the map four animals which look a little
like a pig, a deer, a rhinoceros. and a camel.''

"Yes, and these animals, as well as the
Horse family, would seem to have originated
in North America. But, as we might expect,
these early forms were very generalized, and it
was not until long afterwards that the cameloid
type for example, developed into the true
camel and llama. And here let me say that
we have now reached the culmination of the
Mammal age, and it is not improbable that
across the land-bridge, where to-day is Behring
Strait, the horse, camel, and rhinoceros made
their way into Asia. Marsh tells us that 'an
elevation of only one hundred and eighty feet

wonld close Behring Strait, and give a road
thirty miles wide from America to Asia,   .   .
that such a road did once exist we have much
independent testimony.' "

"And here is an animal that looks a good
deal like a bison," said William.

"Yes, there lived at this period bison whose
horns measured ten feet between tips, and living along with the horse, camel, rhinoceros, and
bison were flesh-eating animals as big as the
present African lion.   It was also at about this
time that the *Mastodon Americanus*, which was
thirteen feet high, appeared in the Mississippi
Valley.   But the genus *Elephas* did not come
until somewhat later.   It is also an interesting
fact, William, that as we are verging towards
the close of the Mammal age, but not earlier,
· we discover in South America, North American
types, and in North America, South American
types, and this would indicate that the Isthmus
of Panama did not rise above the sea until
this period, and it was probably a broader isth-

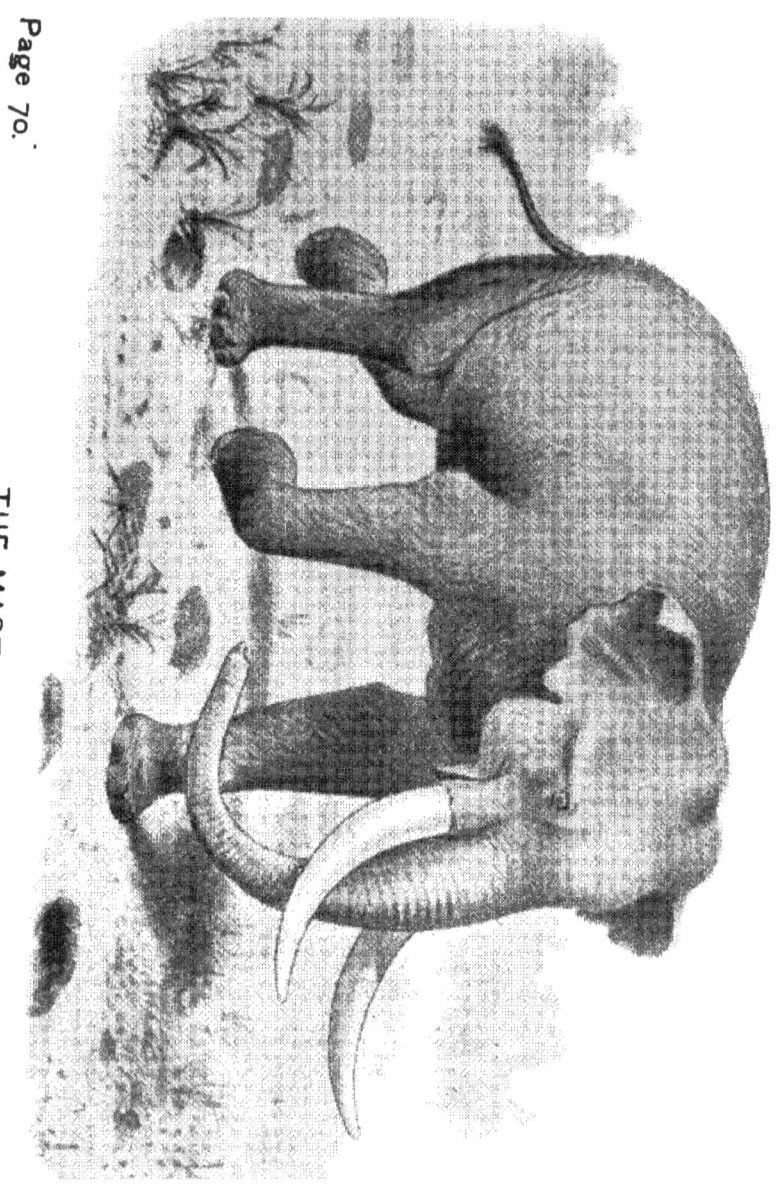

Page 70.

THE MASTADON.

mus then than now. There were, however, mauy peculiar animals in South America long before this epoch, and let me add that the hoofed mammals of South America are extremely isolated, and differ widely from those of North America, while the South American marsupials comprise not only the opossum, but other non-placental forms closely allied to those which have only recently become extinct in Australia; and this fact would seem to render more plausible the theory of a former land connection between Patagonia and the Australian region. Von Zittel, in his learned work, '*The Geological Development of the Mammalia,*' holds it not unreasonable to suppose that South America may, at an early part of the Mammal age, have been connected with South Africa as well as with Australia, and that from these parts of the world it may have received its first mammals.''*

* The late important fossil discoveries in North America by J. L. Wortman, M. D., render it not improbable

"Well, did the Mastodon, Professor, look much like our elephant?"

"Yes, and it differed from it mainly in the character of its teeth, and of all quadrupeds none were at one time more widely distributed over the globe. The mastodon roamed from the tropics to as far as 66° North latitude, and in our own country it survived until a comparatively recent period, and there is reason to believe that it was not unknown to the Indians, who perhaps were the chief cause of its extinction."

"And what is this long, zig-zag streak, Professor, which you have drawn across the age of Mammals?"

I smiled as I answered, "It is meant to

that the peculiar mammals of South America reached there, not by way of Africa or the Australian region, but across the land bridge which must have existed for a brief period during early Eocene time, between North and South America. The key to the Edentate genealogy, therefore, would seem to be found in North America.—See *Bulletin of the American Museum of Natural History, March, 1897.*

represent the Grand Cañon of the Colorado, for it was during this portion of the earth's history that this stupendous geological section was formed. Nowhere else do we behold so mighty an example of the power of erosion. Here for almost three hundred miles the rocky platform has been sawed in two by the Colorado river, to a depth in some places of six thousand feet.''

"It must have taken a long, long time to do that, sir.''

"Yes, William, hundreds of thousands of years, and it was all accomplished by the slow rising up of the land, and by the constant efforts of the water, by sawing down into the rock, to find what is termed the base level of erosion, and the work is still going on.''

"And what is this strange looking animal, Professor, standing on its hind legs and leaning back on its tail?''

"It is the Megatherium, whose remains

have been unearthed in the Pampas of South
America.

"It appeared, as you see, towards the close
of the age of Mammals: in the very last division of it, namely, the Quaternary epoch.
The megatherium was allied to the existing
sloth and ant-eater. It surpassed the rhinoceros
in size, its bones were more massive than the
bones of an elephant, and it must have had an
exceedingly powerful tail; while its fore and
hind limbs were provided with immense claws.
The late Professor Owen's explanation of how
this monster obtained its food, and the use
which it made of its tail, is now generally
accepted as correct. It must have fed on the
leaves of trees, but as probably no tree had
limbs strong enough to support it, it raised
itself on its hind legs, and leaning back on its
tail, pulled the branches towards it. It may
even have been able sometimes to pull a whole
tree down."

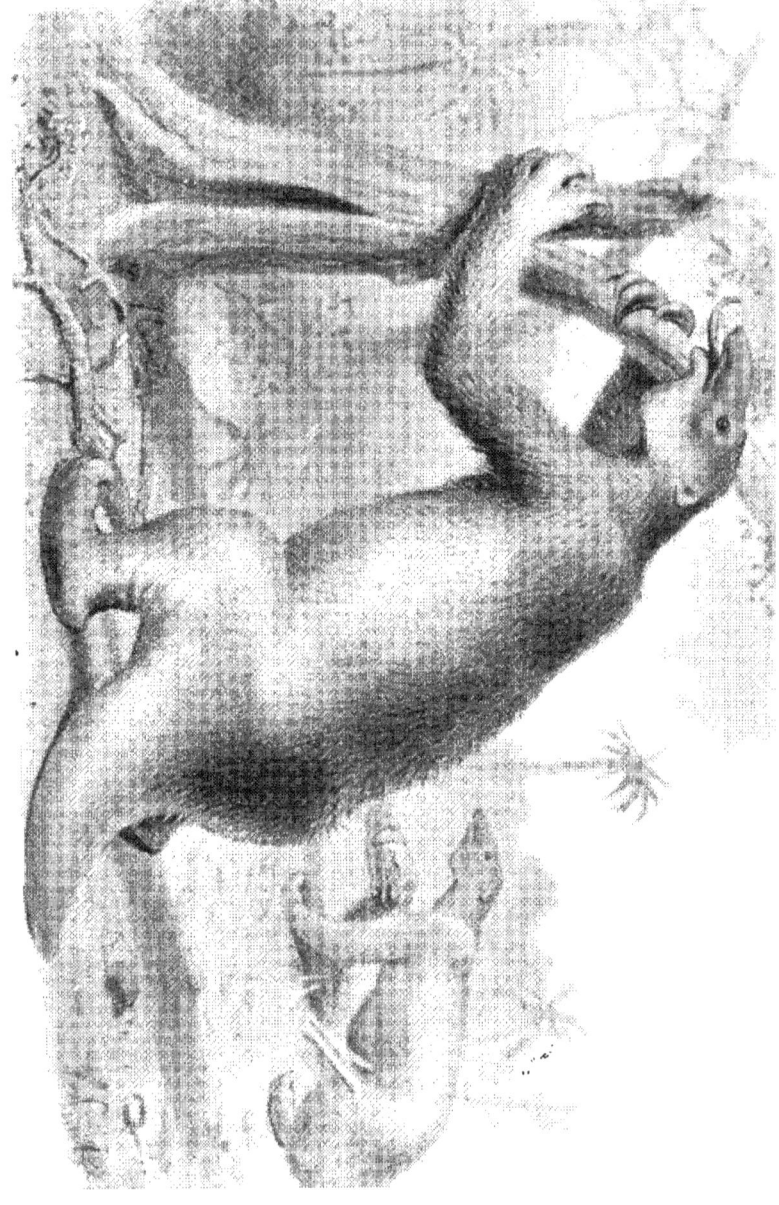

an epoch of cold for our part of the world.
But that time, William, was far back in the
days of the Dinoceras and the Mesohippus.
But since then there have been other periods
when the eccentricity of the earth's orbit was
sufficiently high, combined with the same influence of precession, to have brought about a
Glacial epoch, at least on Dr. Croll's theory.*

"But whatever may have been the cause of
the Ice age, there is evidence to show that at no
very remote period in the past, perhaps not
more than 15,000 years ago, Arctic conditions
prevailed over a part of North America. During the height of the Ice age glaciers would
seem to have covered eastern Canada and New
England, and to have extended in a south-
westerly direction as far as southern Illinois.

---

* Yet Dr. Croll does not wholly discard the influence
of physical agencies. In "*Climate and Cosmology,*"
p. 165, he says: "Eccentricity can produce glaciation only
through means of physical agencies, and for the operation
of these agencies a certain geographical condition of
things is absolutely necessary."

THE MAMMOTH.

Page 81.

From thence they may be traced north-west-ward almost to Montana. There the ice-marks disappear, only to appear again in southern British Columbia; and it is not unlikely that the many small lakes in Minnesota were made by the ice scooping out the rock; and the great lakes, too, may have been mainly formed by the glaciers deepening the original depression which had existed in this part of the continent. During this period northern Europe would seem to have been also covered by hills of ice which spread in the shape of a fan from Scandinavia to as far south as Lyons, while from the Pyre-nees other and smaller glaciers spread towards the north, and the one which rose at Gavarnie and passed over Lourdes has been traced for a distance of thirty-nine miles. It was now that the mammoth, erroneously named *Elephas Primigenius*, came upon the scene, covered with long, thick hair, well suited for cold weather. The musk-ox, an aberrant form allied to the sheep, was also quite common at this time, in regions where to-day it does not exist, owing to the heat; and we find along with the musk-ox and mammoth, the woolly-rhinoceros, while the reindeer then wandered as far south as the frontier of Spain."

"But happily for organic life this dreary epoch was broken by what are termed Inter-glacial periods, and these periods taken together are known among French scientists as the Reindeer age. And what makes the Reindeer age so deeply interesting to us, William, is the fact that by this time God had created Man."

"Indeed! well, how do we know that fact, Professor?"

"Because we find fossil bones, with figures of extinct animals which lived during this period, scratched upon them. The first person in France to call attention to these figures on bone was Desnoyers. As long ago as 1863 he observed them on the remains of *Elephas Meridionalis*, in the neighborhood of Chartres, and near by were a number of flint spear-heads, as

MUSK-OX.

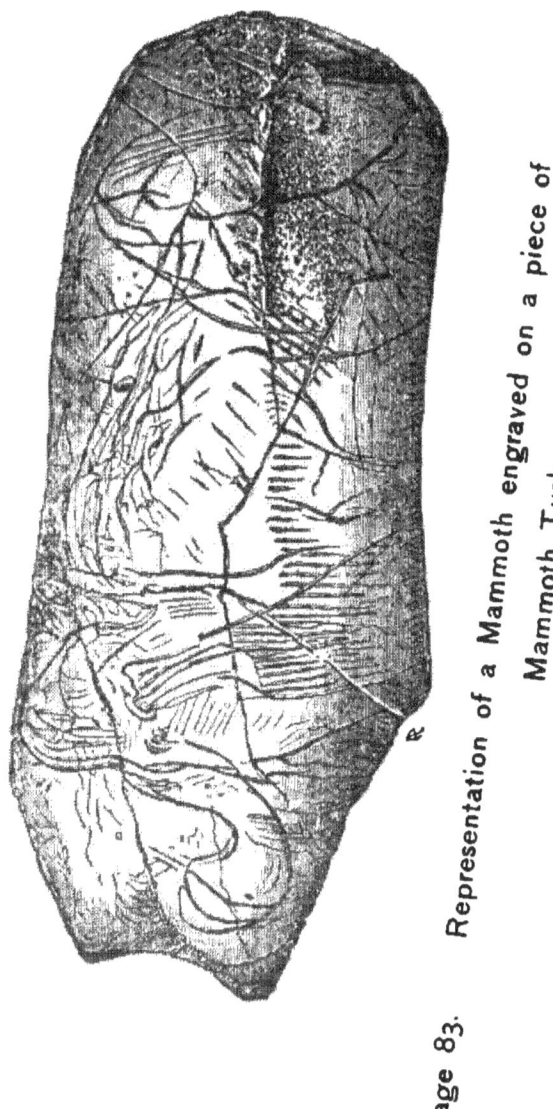

Page 83.

Representation of a Mammoth engraved on a piece of Mammoth Tusk.

well as the skeleton of an hippopotamus. This
discovery, which was made known to the Acad-
emy of Sciences on the eighth of June of that
year, produced a great sensation, and a very
learned man, de Quatrefages, after examining
the bones so interestingly marked, declared that
it was not unreasonable to believe that they
were even older than the Reindeer age, from
the fact that near the remains of the elephant
were remains of the hippopotamus, an animal
which in Europe belonged to an earlier epoch.
In the following year Edouard Lartet discovered in the department of the Dordogne the
first representation of a mammoth. It is engraved on a piece of mammoth tusk, and the
long hair, which is boldly traced, shows that it
is indeed the extinct species *Elephas Primigenius*. Shortly afterwards the Marquis de
Vibraye found in the same part of France, a
piece of reindeer's horn on which is scratched
the head of a mammoth. At about the same
time Peccadeau de l'Isle unearthed in the cave

of Montastuc a reindeer bone on which is represented a reindeer. And among all the prehistoric engravings which I have seen, William, this
is the most finely done. But perhaps the most
precious of all these ancient relics, of which I
mention only a few, is a piece of reindeer bone
on which is represented the figure of a man.
He is in the act of throwing a spear at an
aurochs, which is fleeing with head bent low
and tail high in the air. The engraving is cor-
rectly, even elegantly done. Indeed, a learned
French writer, Emile Cartailhac, says, in *La
France Préhistorique*, ' The Reindeer age is the
artistic period par excellence of all prehistoric
times. . . For the first time man draws,
engraves, carves, represents the living creatures
which surround him with a sense of beauty that
is astonishing. Nor does he forget his own
image.' "

" Well, do you believe that the men who
lived in those days were savages, Professor ?"

" No, I do not believe that our ancestors

of the Inter-glacial periods were necessarily wretched, ignorant people. They may have dwelt in caves; but the caves in France in which arrow heads and human remains have been found, as a rule, face to the south and are near some river, and they must have been warm in winter and cool in the hot inter-glacial summers. Emile Cartailhac, in the above mentioned work, says, 'In the age of which we are speaking game was no doubt more plentiful than in any other, and it was not necessary to go far in order to procure it. The streams were full of fish, life was easy to support. These conditions are not generally found in countries where we have looked for examples of primitive civilization. We believe we should expose ourselves to grave errors, if we compared our ancestors of those times to the miserable tribes which live to-day in the rudest climates and most desolate latitudes.' Nor does it follow, because man then dwelt in caves, that he had no other dwelling places.

He may have had log houses, but these must long since have disappeared. He may also have carved in wood, but this perishable substance would hardly have been preserved to our day, and it is the opinion of de Mortillet, an authority on the subject, that the carvings and engravings of which we have spoken were made with a flint instrument, for flint tools have been found in the same spot with the fossil bones, and they resemble not a little our modern engraving tools. In France the oldest caves which show traces of having been inhabited are the cave of Chelles in the Department of the Seine-et-Marne, the cave of Moustier in the Department of the Dordogne, that of the Madeleine in the same Department, and the cave of Solutré in the department of the Saône-et-Loire. But other and smaller caves have been discovered which are scarcely less interesting. Prof. Bergounoux, in a recent work, *Les Temps Préhistoriques en Quercy*, (Department of the Lot), describes several of these. In the

grotto of Canal he found remains of the reindeer and the horse, a good many bone needles,
as well as several teeth of flesh-eating animals,
which were pierced with a hole, and had no
doubt served as a necklace for some prehistoric
maiden. But the most interesting discovery he
made were some fossil bones, which Prof.
Noulet, Director of the Museum of Natural
History at Toulouse, declared to be the bones
of a very little dog, and if the Professor is not
mistaken, then *Canis Familiaris* was among
the animals made use of by our early fore-
fathers. And here let me say, William, that I
myself have seen along the river Loire, in
France, a number of comfortable, well fur-
nished caverns, and I have a friend whose
home is in one of these rocky abodes.''

"I should like very much to see his cave,
Professor.''

"Well, some day, William, we may go to
France together, and then we shall make this
modern cave-dweller a visit. His home, which

is only a few miles from Tours, and near the
ancient monastery of Marmoutier, will surprise
you by its convenient arrangement and ele-
gant furniture, and I hope that I may always
be as comfortably housed as he is."

CHAPTER V.

"In our last conversation, William, I told you that we have good evidence to show that early man lived at the same time as the mammoth."

"Yes, and I hope, sir, that you have a great deal more to tell me. It is so interesting."

"Well, I have something more to say, William, but it does not relate to the past history of the earth, for with man God's glorious work culminated. I have done my best, by representing on a sheet of paper an ideal section of rock, with the different geological ages marked upon it, and also a few of their characteristic fossils, to give you a bird's-eye view of the Past; and in the study of the rocks from

the lowest and the oldest to the highest and the
newest, we recognize on every page of the
record the wisdom of the Creator. We see the
life-system alter many times, but new types
come upon the scene only when the proper
time arrives, when the earth is fitted to receive
them. When one epoch is drawing to a close,
in the slowly changing organisms, in the transition forms, we perceive anticipations of the
epoch that is coming; and it is certainly interesting to observe how the fossil species from
two consecutive strata are much nearer of kin
to each other than are the fossil species from
strata which are further apart. But as I have
said, William, it was vitally necessary for animated nature to vary as surrounding conditions
varied. It was either that or extinction. But
the Creator has wisely allowed organic life to
put itself, according to certain laws, in harmony
with the environment. Palaeontology, classi-
fication, geographical distribution, and Embry-

ology * furnish overwhelming converging evidence that during the course of the earth's life-history all animals with the exception of a few persistent types, have been slowly changing as climates and geography have changed, and it is the common belief of naturalists—men who have made Nature a special study—that the animals which lived millions of years ago are the ancestors (not however always in a direct line) of the ones which are living to-day."

"What a grand picture it is," exclaimed William. Then after a pause: "But now, Professor, before you begin to tell me anything more, do give me a definition of species."

"Well, there are several definitions, William, but before I give you any of them let me remark that no word is so difficult to define as the word—species. Throughout animated na-

---

* The science of Comparative Embryology, as a rule, gives the family history repeated in the individual history: it is considered to-day by the best authorities as the principal witness to the theory of continuous descent with adaptive modifications.

ture the process of transmutation is exceedingly
finely graduated, and it is an undeniable fact
that the more our knowledge of animals and
plants increases, the more intermediate forms,
living as well as fossil, do we discover. Few
persons who are not naturalists know how uni-
versally plants and animals are varying; and
varieties may be viewed as incipient species,
species as incipient genera, genera as incipient
families. But at what precise moment they
cease to be the one and become the other,
where is the exact dividing line, it would be
almost impossible to determine. However, to
come back to a definition of species, this is what
Lamarck, an eminent French scientist, says,
‘ A species is a collection of similar individuals,
which are perpetuated by generation in the
same condition, as long as their environment
has not changed sufficiently to bring about variation in their habits, their character, and their
form.’   Or you may take this other definition
by Professor Albert Gaudry, in his recent work,

*Essai de Paléontologie Philosophique.** A
' species is an assemblage of individuals which
are not yet sufficiently differentiated as to cease
to be fertile when crossed.' "

" Well, Professor, I prefer Prof. Gaudry's
definition. It is shorter," said William.

" And now, my boy, while I close what I
have called the book of the rocks, let me repeat, and let me urge you not to forget that
this book, despite its many lost leaves, reveals
to us on the whole an unfolding, a progressive
development of organic life from the simple to
the complex, from low to higher forms. A
geologist can tell by the stage of a fossil's development to what epoch in the world's history
it belongs. If, for example, you show him
two fossil birds, say Archaeopteryx and Ichthyornis, one of which is more reptilian, less typi-
cally bird-like than the other, he knows at once

* L'espèce est l'assemblage des individus qui ne sont
pas encore assez différenciés pour cesser de donner ensem-
ble des produits féconds.

that it has been found in lower strata, and belongs to an older geological formation. Bear
in mind also, that as we advance in time animals
become more active as well as more intelligent.
The primitive fishes had beneath their armor
soft, cartilaginous skeletons, and their tails were
so constructed that they could not give the
strong blows necessary for rapid swimming.
The early quadrupeds, as we know, were reptiles, clumsy brutes with little muscular energy,
and which passed their existence crawling over
soft, swampy land. We know, too, that the
foot of Eohippus, the ancestral horse, only six-
teen inches high, was infinitely less adapted to
swift locomotion than the foot of Equus, its
far-off descendant. And the same rule holds
good with regard to the five senses : they all
become more developed with the progress of
time. No doubt, judging by fossil remains,
the early reptiles had pretty good eyesight, but
it was not equal to that of the birds which
came after them. The sense of hearing has

also grown more acute. In the primeval days
what little earth had risen above the water was
comparatively a silent earth; but by and by
insects appeared to chirp and to hum, and to be
answered by other insects, and this humming
and chirping was followed later on by the bel-
lowing and roaring of mammals, and by the
sweet voices of the birds. Along the narrow
coast lines of the emerging continents there was
little or no vegetation, no flowers, no blossoms
to give perfume to the sandy wastes: it was
the reign of invertebrates, and among invertebrates, the sense of smell is scarcely developed.
But with vertebrates, animals with a backbone,
came nostrils. Yet the earliest vertebrates, as
we know, were fishes, and among fishes the
sense of smell made only a feeble step in advance. But with the continued growth of the
continents appeared amphibians. Their sense
of smell, however, is less developed than among
true reptiles, while among these it is less developed than among mammals, and we all know

how perfect to-day this sense is among some
mammals, especially the dog. As for man, he
is not content with nature's perfumes, he must
needs make artificial ones to tickle his sense of
smell. In regard to the sense of taste, as the
organs on which it depends are not capable of
being fossilized, it is only by analogy that we
may infer that it has also developed with time.
As in our age we see insects and molluscs
among whom the organs of taste are not distinctly marked, nevertheless selecting their
food, so we may infer that among the primeval
invertebrates this sense did at least exist. But
we know that fishes, which were the first vertebrates, have a dull sense of taste, nor is this
sense much more developed among reptiles.
But mammals, which appear at a later geological age, possess, at least many of them, a very
delicate sense of taste. We need not say how
fastidious some of our domestic animals are
about their food, nor how civilized man grum-
bles when his meals are not properly prepared,

The sense of touch has likewise developed with
time. This is indicated by the study of fossil
remains. The ancestral fishes and reptiles were
encased in armor, and hence their breasts and
bellies did not feel the want of this sense. But,
excepting the Dinosaurs and crocodiles, the
reptiles of a later epoch were not armor clad,
and it is probable that their sense of touch was
somewhat keener; yet among the reptiles of
our own age this sense is very imperfect. Even
most of the early mammals were thick-skinned
brutes, Pachyderms, as Cuvier called them,
among whom the sense of touch was not near
so delicate as among the mammals of to-day;
while man, the highest and noblest of all mammals, possesses this sense in the utmost degree
of perfection. But if the five senses have
developed with time, so have the sentiments of
love and hate. Even to-day the maternal feel-
ings are not very strong among invertebrates,
while fishes, which as we know were the first
vertebrates, take little or no care of their

young. * Nor can we doubt that the intelligence of living organisms has gone on increasing with time. The brain cavities of the early
reptiles were exceedingly small, and the same
was true of the early mammals. But often-
times their bodies were immense, and for what
I am telling you in regard to increased activity
of body and development of the senses, I refer
you to the works of the American scientists,
Marsh, Cope, and Leidy, and also to Prof.
Albert Gaudry's recent work, *Essai de Paléontologie Philosophique.* And now, William,
having finished what I have to say about the
earth's history as contained in the book of the
rocks, let me tell you something about the
earth as it is to-day. And to begin, you must
know that comparatively little of it is dry land,
almost three-quarters of it is water. Around
the poles we find a dreary waste of ice, every-
thing there is solitude and silence. But there

---

* To this rule there are marked exceptions; the dace
and the stickleback show strong family feeling.

is evidence to show that this was not always the case. Indeed, the French naturalist Buffon believed that on our planet, which was slowly cooled and consolidated, life began at the poles, and that from thence it spread in the direction of the tropics, where at first the heat was too intense to admit of any kind of life. But it is only within recent years that we have been able to get a glimpse of the ancient Arctic zone, which is much more accessible than the Antarctic, and what has thus far been brought to light makes Buffon's daring conjecture appear not so very improbable. In Spitzbergen and Greenland, in Alaska, along the banks of the Mackenzie River, even in Grinnell Land, between 80° and 83° North Latitude, fossil plants have been found belonging to the far-off period of the Dinosaurs and earliest mammals, and these plants,—among which are the swamp cypress, magnolia, elm, birch, poplar, and laurel—have been described by Prof. Oswald Heer, of Zurich, in his admirable work, *Flora*

Fossilis Arctica.   But steadily the cold which
had set in within the Arctic circle towards the
close of the Reptile age went on increasing.
A season of snow became more definitely
marked, and slowly but surely the flora adapted
itself to changed conditions, until at length it
turned into a purely Arctic flora.   But while
recent discoveries, William, have proved that
Greenland (which in a former period might
have been called a continent, for it touched
Spitzbergen on the east and south, took in Iceland, perhaps even included Scotland, while to
the north it stretched beyond 82°) was the
original native home of an abundant vegetation,
scientists are not agreed as to what brought
about so marked a change of climate.   Some
would explain the high temperature which once
prevailed from the poles to the tropics, by the
greater central heat of our globe.   But in an-
swer to this it has been said that the caloric
contained within the central nucleus must soon
have ceased to exert any marked influence over

the earth's surface. We know that the outer
portion of a lava flood even several yards thick,
soon cools and solidifies. Prof. Heer, in the
introduction to his work on fossil plants, which
we have mentioned, puts forth the hypothesis
that our earth is carried by the sun around a
central star, buried in the depths of space, and
that in accomplishing this inconceivably immense cycle of a year, whose seasons must be
measured by myriads of centuries, we pass
through alternate regions of great heat and
great cold. But he gives no valid reason for
supposing that there are different temperatures
in different parts of stellar space, and his theory
has not found many supporters. Another
hypothesis, which is held by good authorities,
refers variations of climate to the combined
effects of the precession of the equinoxes and
changes in the eccentricity of the earth's orbit,
and about this I have already spoken to you.
While other authorities, as you know, would
explain climatic variations by geographical

changes—by a different distribution of land
and water. But whatever may have brought
about variations of climate, there is certainly a
high probability that at one time, not very remote, geologically speaking, the poles were
devoid of snow and ice."

"Well, you say, Professor, that almost
three-quarters of the earth is covered by water :
pray, how deep is the ocean, and what may its
bottom look like?"

"The average depth of the ocean, William,
is somewhat more than two miles, or let us say
that it is twice as far below the shore line as
Mt. Washington is above it. But the very
deepest soundings which have been obtained
(and these are in the north-west Pacific, off the
coast of Japan) have reached a depth of five
miles and a quarter. As to what the bottom
of the ocean is like, I should say that a bird's-
eye view of the Atlantic would show us the
Island of Porto Rico towering up to a great
height, like a mountain of the Himalayas : the

Bermudas would appear like an isolated Alp not quite so high, with several peaks; while the Azores would resemble the topmost part of an extensive plateau, a thousand miles broad from east to west; and this area of comparatively shallow water, which begins at Iceland and runs far to the southward, divides the North Atlantic into two valleys, an eastern and a western. The Gulf of Mexico, in this bird's-eye view, would take the appearance of a great depression, more than two miles deep, bounded on the south by a ridge of sand extending from Yucatan to Key West, and with an opening leading into the Caribbean Sea, while the latter would assume the form of another depression not quite so deep. And here let me observe that the latest soundings made by the U. S. Coast Survey reveal the interesting fact that the Gulf of Mexico may be characterized as an almost tideless American Mediterranean. The slope of the continent runs for a long distance below the sea level before it reaches the lowest

part of the Gulf, which, as I have said, is over
two miles deep, while a curve of little more than
six hundred feet below the surface stretches
almost from Yucatan to the extremity of
Florida. It is also interesting to find how
many of the West India Islands are separated
by water very little more than three-quarters
of a mile deep, and this comparatively shallow
space would make Jamaica the end of a great
promontory. In regard to the Atlantic as it
exists to-day, good authorities believe that it is
not a very old sea, and that it has undergone
marked changes. The Pacific, on the contrary, is an extremely ancient body of water,
and its general outlines, according to geological
observations, were probably determined not
later than the Carboniferous epoch, which, as
you remember, closes the age of Invertebrates.
The bottom of this vast ocean from Peru to
Kamtschatka, may be described as an almost
unbroken plain, covered by from a little more
than two to a little more than three miles of

water. But when we approach the coast of
Asia, and are on a line between the Aleutian
Islands and Japan, we come to a valley in the
ocean bed 7,500 feet deep: and it is not likely
the sounding lead will discover a deeper depression than this."

"And do fishes live at those great depths,
Professor?"

"A few may wander there occasionally,
William. But believe me, despite the fanciful
pictures which some writers have drawn of the
ocean bed, its desolation in the deepest parts
must be extreme. Beyond the first mile it is a
vast desert of slime and ooze, upon which is
constantly dripping a rain of dead carcasses
from the surface, which carcasses supply the
nourishment for the scanty fauna inhabiting
the abyssal region several miles from the sunshine, and the microscope reveals that the
slimy matter covering the deep sea bed is very
similar in composition to the ancient chalk of
the Cretaceous or Chalk period, which period

closes the age of Reptiles, while mixed with it here and there are minute metallic and magnetic bodies, which have been proved to be dust from meteorites. At long intervals a phosphorescent light may be seen gleaming from the head of some passing fish, which has strayed hither from a higher and happier zone. But when this light vanishes awful darkness returns, nor is it until we have mounted pretty far toward the surface that the scene changes for the better. We now begin to meet with forests of brilliantly colored sponges, while the phosphorescent animals swimming about have become more numerous; and the higher we rise the more living things do we meet, until at length the scene becomes truly animated. When only 1200 feet separate us from the sunshine we come upon the first seaweed and kelp (1200 feet is the deepest limit of plant life in the ocean). But we must continue still to mount, and get as near the surface as 120 feet, before we find any coral-polyps. As plants do not live in the very deep sea, the deep sea animals either prey on one another or get their food from dead organisms which sink down to them. Capt. Maury of the U. S. Navy, whose book, *Physical Geography of the Sea*, is well worth reading, says: ' The sea, like the snow cloud with its flakes in a calm, is always letting fall upon its bed showers of microscopic shells.' And experiment proves that a tiny shell would take about a week to sink from the surface to the deepest part : and since the sunlight does not penetrate much beyond nine hundred feet, there would be perpetual darkness there, except for phosphorescence. Many animals inhabiting very deep water have rudimentary eyes. But these blind creatures have long feelers, which help them to grope their way along the bottom. Other deep-sea animals, on the contrary, have enormous eyes, and these very likely congregate around such of their number as are phosphorescent, and they may perhaps follow these moving lanterns

about wherever they go; and so bright is this
phosphorescent light on many of the fish
brought up by the dredge, that during the
brief space the animals survive it is not difficult to read by it."

CHAPTER VI.

THE AGE OF MAMMALS.—Continued.

"Is it not strange, Professor, that animals are able to live at such great depths in the sea as they do? is not the pressure at times enormous?"

"Yes, William, the pressure may be several tons to the square inch; but the reason why fishes and molluscs living three miles and more under water can bear this pressure, is that they have exceedingly loose tissues, which allow the water to pass through every part of them, and thus to equalize the weight; when the pressure is removed they perish. In the Challenger expedition, sent out by the British Government, all the sharks brought up from a depth of a little less than three-quarters of a mile, were dead when they got to the surface."

" Well, I suppose, Professor, that most of the animals inhabiting the sea prefer to live not very far from the sunshine? "

" Yes, as a rule the phosphorescent animals seem to like a depth not greater than 900 feet, where they drift about as the winds and waves list. But if there are wanderers in the sea without any fixed abode, other animals apparently live and die on the spot where they were born. Many of the blind fish of the very deep sea have burrowing habits and live buried in the mud. Perhaps the most curious deep-sea fish discovered is the *Gastrostomus Bairdii*, which gets its food by doing nothing except keep open its enormous mouth, into which the water and the organisms it contains pours. Only its head protrudes above the ooze of the bottom ; its fins are atrophied, and its power to move about is extremely limited, if indeed it ever moves."

"Well, Professor, where does the Red Sea get its name from? "

"From a tiny seaweed of a blood-red tint, which affeċts the color of the water. We find the same weed in some parts of the west coast of South America, and Alex. Agassiz, during calm weather, observed it in the Gulf of Mexico."

"And please tell me, sir, what is the Sargasso Sea?"

"It is a broad stretch of water in the middle of the South Atlantic, which used to be the dread of old navigators, who, when the wind was light, could with difficulty make their way through it, for its surface is a mass of tough and tangled seaweed,—a floating prairie—about a thousand miles broad; and it, as well as the floating prairies found in the Pacific, are looked upon as the survivors of a vastly larger field of seaweed which was swept round the globe by the equatorial current in a former geological epoch. And let me add that it is in the Sargasso Sea we find that interesting little fish *Antennarius*, provided with uncommonly long

fore fins, which enable it to cling to the seaweed, out of which it builds for its eggs a nest
not unlike a bird's nest.''

"Well, I am curious to know, Professor,
how naturalists have been able to learn so much
about the deep sea and the animals living
in it.''

"By dredging and sounding, William.
For this purpose rope was at first used. But
a new era dawned for deep sea study when,
in 1872, Sir William Thompson invented a
machine in which wire took the place of hemp.
But he would hardly know his own invention
with the great improvements made in it by
Lieutenant-Commander Sigsbee, U. S. N.
Sigsbee's machine is quite accurate for the
deepest soundings, and the moment the sinker
touches bottom the wire ceases to run out, and
the dropping of the shot is detected on deck
with unerring certainty. The advantage of
steel wire in dredging is the speed with which
the dredge can be lowered and hoisted. On

the Challenger expedition the best part of a day was spent in lifting the dredge from a depth somewhat less than two miles. On the Blake several hauls a day were made from a greater depth. But if you wish to learn more about the ocean and its inhabitants, William, you cannot do better than read Prof. Alex. Agassiz's, *Three Cruises of the U. S. Coast Survey Steamer Blake.*"

"I shall certainly read that book, Professor. And now do tell me something about the Gulf Stream: I have heard it so often mentioned."

"Well, of all the currents of the ocean none has been so closely studied, and none is of more importance to climate. If the Gulf Stream were to disappear (and only the Isthmus of Panama, 27 1-2 miles broad at the narrowest part, keeps it in its track), the effect on Europe would be marked: a lower temperature would surely follow. This benign stream, which is equal to a river 50 miles broad and 1000 feet deep, is caused by the trade winds; and the

first chart of it was published by Benjamin
Franklin, who learned of its existence from
Nantucket whalemen.   The whole body of the
Atlantic within the influence of these winds
may be said to be moving slowly westward,
until at length having struck the coast of South
America, a portion of this great mass of water
is deflected to the north and into the Caribbean
Sea and thence into the Gulf of Mexico, where
the pent-up current, rising more than three
feet above the general level, forms, as it were,
a hill of water, from which springs the Gulf
Stream proper.   The velocity of the stream at
St. Augustine, Florida, is four miles an hour.
But as it flows to the northward and eastward,
assuming more and more the shape of a fan, its
velocity decreases as its breadth increases, until
off Newfoundland it is less than two miles an
hour.   The marked influence which its warm
water has in carrying to a high latitude the
animals of a southern region, was shown by
the dredgings of the U. S. Fish Commission :

many fish were brought up off the coast of New England that were characteristic of the West Indies. But let me observe, William, that if Franklin was the first to make known to the world the existence of the Gulf Stream, it should not be forgotten that the existence of a flow of warm surface water from the equator toward the poles, and a compensating cold under-current returning to the equator, was maintained several centuries ago by a learned Italian, Leonardo da Vinci." Here I paused a moment and looked at William, who was sitting with his face buried in his hands. " Are you tired?" I said wonderingly.

" Tired! Oh no, indeed, Professor, I am listening with all my ears, and wishing that you had to begin all over again, for what you have told me about the past history of the earth has awakened in me an unspeakable desire to know more; and I want to learn, too, as much as I can about the animals and plants which are living to-day."

"Well, believe me, William, there is no study which so quickens our powers of observation as the study of natural history: it is like strolling through Wonderland, with no end to the beauties and the marvels which spring up on every side of us."

"True, true," exclaimed William. "And now, Professor, do tell me something about Australia, that big island so far away, and which you once called by such an odd name: you called it the fossil continent."

"Well, Australia, William, which extends from 39° to 11° South latitude, and which is separated from the Indo-Malay region by a narrow but deep belt of water, is held by good authorities to equal, from a zoological point of view, all the rest of the earth. Its separation from the mainland of Asia probably dates from far back in the age of Reptiles, and no country has changed so little during later geological time: Australia would seem to have stood still and been forgotten, while the rest of the earth has developed and assumed a new fauna and flora. Its mammals especially (excepting the bats and small rodents such as rats and mice) are markedly isolated: they represent types which at one time were broadly distributed over the earth, but which have now become extinct everywhere except here and in a few of the outlying islands, with the single exception of the opossum in distant America. And let me say, William, that this wide disconnuity is a sign of great antiquity. To quote the words of a well-known naturalist, Alfred R. Wallace, in his interesting book, *Island Life*, 'The more widely the fragments are scattered the more ancient we may usually presume the parent group to be.' And now picture to yourself a country almost as large as Europe without any of the forms from which domestic animals have descended, unless we except the dingo, the native dog, which is not a marsupial, and which is believed to have been introduced by man. This isolated, lost land, no doubt

millions of years separated from its parent continent, possesses a life-system so uncommonly
primitive and peculiar that naturalists have
agreed to make Australia a separate region.
We meet here with two new Orders, namely,
Marsupials and Monotremes, which are represented no where else excepting, as I have said,
by the opossum in America. Now, these
animals are the lowest in organization of all
mammals, as well as the earliest to appear in
geological time. By a Marsupial I mean an
animal whose embryonic development is com-
pleted outside the body of the parent, in a
pouch, *marsupium*, into which the mother
places her immature young.

"A Monotreme, William, is a mammal
whose intestinal, generative, and urinary organs
· open into one and the same cloaca or cavity,
after the manner of reptiles and birds. The
marsupial bones are present, but not the marsupial pouch, and this creature is looked upon
as even lower in organization than a marsupial:

indeed a Monotreme would appear to stand at the very base of the mammalian series, and from its affinity to birds and reptiles we might consider it as only nascent mammalian. Among marsupials the largest is the kangaroo, in whose pouch are found several long string-like pieces of flesh, and after the mother, in an almost mysterious manner, has transferred the blind and naked little thing, no bigger than a human baby's finger, into the pouch and stuck it on one of these milk strings, she presses the milk into its mouth by the help of a peculiar muscle, and the larynx of the young one is so constructed that it is able to breathe while it is thus nourished, without any danger of choking."

"Well, do all marsupials resemble a kangaroo, Professor?"

"Certainly not, William. The opossum, you know, is a marsupial; and they not only vary greatly in looks but also in habits. Some are as small as a mouse and go on all-fours;

others move on their hind legs alone; some eat grass and leaves, others live on meat, insects, and honey. But in all marsupials the brain development is extremely small. They manifest little if any affection for their offspring, and the female kangaroo has been known to throw her young one out of the pouch when she is closely pursued by the hounds. The most intelligent of Australian marsupials is the opossum; and it is interesting to kuow, William, that the American opossum is the most highly organized of the marsupial Order."

"Indeed!" exclaimed William. "Well, hereafter I shall look on our opossum with some respect."

"The Australian flying-squirrel," I continued, "is closely related to the opossum, and the smallest of the family, which is not bigger than a mouse, is able to skim through the air and alight with accuracy at a point eighty paces away. The so-called Australian bear is quite a harmless marsupial, whose food is grass, and

it is in no way related to the Bear family.
When its young one is old enough to quit the
pouch, it perches itself on the mother's back
and goes about with her wherever she goes.
But the marsupial tiger is a carniverous beast,
fierce and very destructive to sheep and young
cattle. As I have said, William, the monotremes are even lower in organization than the
marsupials; they are a dwindling group, con-
sisting only of the ornithorynchus or duck
mole, and the echidna or native hedgehog.

"The ornithorhynchus, whose teeth disappear before it attains its growth, is possessed of
jaws very like the bill of a duck. Its body is
fifteen inches long, and the feet are webbed.
The echidna also swims well, but its feet are
not webbed. Now remember, William, that
these two mammals, which burrow under
ground, exceed in strangeness any other animals in existence. Their skulls, as in the case
of birds, are devoid of sutures, while the front
extremities are joined to the breast bone by

what is termed a coracoid and an epi-coracoid,
the same as in reptiles.   But the strangest fact
connected with the monotremes is that they do
not bring forth young alive, but lay eggs, and
after the young one emerges from the shell it is
suckled by the mother.   The eggs, moreover,
in their stages of development are very like the
eggs of reptiles, and outwardly resemble those
of a turtle, and it is held by good authorities
that these low-type mammals clearly point to a
reptilian ancestry.   Nor are the birds of Australia, William, less interesting than the mammals.   The jungle-hen and the brush-turkey
construct with their powerful feet a mound
of earth and fallen leaves in which to bury
their eggs, where, reptile-like, they are hatched
by the artificial heat generated by the ferment-
ing of vegetable and other refuse matter.   But
it has only lately been discovered how the
young birds get out of the mound; they lie
on their backs and work their way to the surface with their feet.   Wallace, in his book

entitled *Geographical Distribution of Animals*, speaking of this curious mode of hatching eggs says, ' This may perhaps be an adaptation to the peculiar condition of so large a portion of Australia in respect to long droughts and scanty water supply entailing a periodical scarcity of all kinds of food. In such a country the confinement of the parents to one spot during the long period of incubation would often lead to starvation and the consequent death of the offspring. Another curious bird, William, is the bower-bird. It is about as big as a thrush, and is noted for the opening or bower which it makes in the brushwood, but which is never used as a nest. It clears the dead leaves and twigs off the ground for the space of two or three square feet, and in this clearing it deposits heaps of snail shells and red berries, or it will sometimes arrange a number of fresh leaves side by side, and at these little heaps of bright colored objects and rows of green leaves it gazes and sings for ever so long; then when

the leaves begin to wither and the shells lose
their brightness, the bird stops singing and sets
to work gathering new ones. It really seems
to enjoy looking at its playthings. And why
not ? The same God that made man made this
little bird."

"Well, Professor, I should like to go to
Australia just to see the bower-bird."

"It would certainly be worth seeing, William. There is also a singular fish, the Ceratodus, found in South Australia. It is looked
upon as a survival from a past geological epoch,
for its fossil remains have been discovered in
strata belonging to the age of Reptiles. It is
near of kin to the primitive lung-fish, which
had lungs as well as gills; but the ceratodus
has only one lung. Its brain presents an embryonic condition, and in its anatomy we find a
resemblance to salamanders. At night it sometimes leaves the water and feeds on herbage
near the river bank, for its fins are so constructed that it is able to wobble along like a

tortoise; and it appears not improbable that from this fish may have descended some of the earlier amphibians. And here let me say, William, that whenever a species has a very local range, when it does not exist outside of a certain narrow limit, it is a sign that it is verging toward extinction.''

CHAPTER VII.

THE AGE OF MAMMALS.—Continued.

" Please tell me, Professor, what is meant by mimicry in natural history?"

" Well, this expression, William, is misleading. When, in natural history, we speak of one species of animal imitating another species, and putting on a disguise so perfect that it is hard at first to tell the two apart, when we say it mimics, it is owing to the poverty of our language to find a better word. For the deceptive resemblance is not a conscious act—although I myself believe that some kind of dim intelligence may have helped the ancestral form to profit by the initial likeness—but is supposed by good authorities to have been brought about by a variety of one kind having originally borne a superficial likeness to another

which was gifted with special means of protection, and in consequence of this fortunate likeness which had a tendency to be reproduced,
the former was able to escape from its enemies.
The imitation may have been very slight in the
beginning; but as time went on, in the course
of generations, it became more and more com-
plete, by the variety which more closely resembled the species imitated being naturally preserved, while those which had not the disguise
perished. In Brazil, for instance, the Heliconidae butterflies, which most birds will not
touch on account of their nasty odor and taste,
are closely mimicked by another kind of butterfly belonging to the genus Leptalis: and the
latter so adroitly mimics the Heliconidae in
form, color, and mode of flight, that it is only
after a careful examination that one is able to
discover the essential differences. But the
birds believe that it is a butterfly of a bad tast-
ing kind, and avoid it: keen-sighted as they
are, they are thoroughly deceived. There is

also in Brazil a big caterpillar, which so closely
imitates a poisonous viper that it frightens you
when it draws back as if to strike. It is also
quite probable, William, that the resemblance
which some animals bear to their environment,
and which is called *protective coloration*, has
been brought about in the same way. For this
resemblance cannot be explained by the direct
action of climate or soil. In the Arctic regions
white is the color which best protects, by making the animal of the same hue as the landscape.
Accordingly we find the polar bear white, the
only bear that is white. The Alpine hare,
the ermine, and the Arctic fox turn white in
the snowy season. Among birds the ptarmigan
in winter loses its summer plumage, which har-
monizes so well with the lichen-covered stones
among which it hides, and turns white, so very
white that one may tramp through a flock lying
in the snow without perceiving a single bird.
The difficulty which some persons find in recon-
ciling seasonal imitations with the hypothesis of

natural selection, is explained by Romanes in his book entitled, *Darwin and after Darwin*. He says, ' Natural selection is not supposed to act always in the same manner, and if, as in the case of a regularly recurring change in the colors of the environment, correspondingly recurrent changes are required to appear in the colors of the animal, natural selection sets its premium upon those individuals, the constitutions of which best lend themselves to seasonal changes of the needful kind, probably under the influence of stimuli supplied by the changes of external conditions (temperature, moisture, etc.).' "

"But, Professor, how comes it that the raven, which in midwinter goes as far north as any known bird or beast, remains black?"

" Because it feeds on carrion and therefore has no need of concealment in order to get near its prey."

" And are lions and tigers colored as they are because it is beneficial to them?"

"This is the better opinion, William. The lion by its sandy color easily conceals itself by crouching on the desert sand, while the stripes of the tiger assimilate well with the vertical stems of the bamboo and tall, stiff grass of the jungle. Even an animal as big as a giraffe is said by travelers to be admirably concealed by its form and color when standing perfectly still among the dead trees which are often found on the outskirts of the groves where it feeds. Its spots, its long neck, the peculiar shape of its head and horns appear altogether so like broken branches that even the natives have been known to mistake a tree for a giraffe and a giraffe for a tree. In regard to the coloring of birds, William, the naturalists believe that the dull colors of the female have been acquired for protection while sitting on the nest. To this rule there are exceptions, as the kingfishers, toucans, parrots, and starlings, in which both sexes are equally conspicuous. But these birds either nest in holes or build dome-shaped nests, which hide the sitting bird."

"But, Professor, how do you explain the fact that in some species of birds the female is actually more conspicuously colored than the male?"

"In these few curious cases, William, such as the dotterel and one or two others, it is found that the relation of the sexes in regard to nesting is reversed; here the male bird sits on the eggs, while the more attractive but pugnacious female stands exposed to the enemy's eye."

"Well, it seems to me, Professor, that the conspicuous colors of some animals, the skunk for example, ought certainly to be a detriment."

"On the contrary, William, the coloring of the skunk adds to its safety. The bushy white tail curved well up over its black and white body is a signal to attract attention; it is an advertisement, a warning. In the dusk this

white signal is pretty sure to be seen, and pre-
vents this bold, presuming little creature from
being pounced upon by any of the night-prowl-
ing Carnivora, who wisely and quickly turn
aside the instant they recognize it.   Indeed,
we have in the skunk one of the very best examples of what is known as *warning coloration*.   And bear in mind, William, that it is
the belief of most naturalists that warning
coloration, protective coloration, and mimicry
have all been brought about by what may be
termed the process of discrimination of variations : that is to say, by the survival of those
variations which are most in harmony with
surrounding conditions—with the environment.
In the case of the skunk, for example, the animal whose colors in the ancestral form varied
ever so little in the direction of safety, would
naturally have some slight advantage and more
chances to survive.   And then through heredity, variability, and the continuous process of
discrimination, the at first slightly warning

colors would, generation after generation slowly, surely incline to become more conspicuous and perfect, until in the end they became what they are to-day."

"How wonderful!" exclaimed William.

"Yes, truly wonderful, my boy." Yet see what man, who has not worked nearly so long as Nature, has been able by following the same process of discrimination to accomplish in a comparatively brief time; among many other things, from the common wild crab-apple, man has produced the Golden Pippin." With these words I rose from the bed of moss which had been our resting place for so many happy hours, and as William followed my example, he said :

"I wish, Professor, that we might begin over again our interesting talks about Nature."

To this I replied :

"I hope, William, that the knowledge which I have been able to impart may awaken in you a desire to learn more about the animals

and plants which are in existence to-day.
Nature is a wonderland filled with beauties and
curiosities, and to explore this wonderland will
stimulate and quicken your mental powers as
nothing ever did before. The faculty of obser-
·vation will be thoroughly aroused, and you will
learn, perhaps for the first time, to observe,
compare, and contrast. And, moreover, by
developing a fondness for Nature, may not
some young persons be made less cruel to the
birds and beasts around them? Almighty God
has put them here to serve us, but we should
not be heartless masters. And if, as the distinguished naturalist Wallace says, we are living in a zoologically impoverished world, from
which all the hugest and fiercest and strangest
forms have recently disappeared, it is no less
true that the day is approaching, it is not very
far off, when through the influence of man,
the elephant, the giraffe, the rhinoceros, even
the deer and the bear, as well as many of the
birds whose sweet notes give us joy, will be

ntterly extinct: aye, it is probable that in
another hundred years nearly all our wild animals will be found only in museums. Therefore, William, let us enjoy dear Nature as
much as we can, and let us put off, as far as
in our power lies, the unromantic day when the
forests will all be cut down, the running brooks
dried up, and when there will be nothing left
for the eye to rest upon but civilization."